THE FOUR LIVES OF J. S. FREEMAN

Book Two

CITIZEN

Yvonne Anderson

THE FOUR LIVES OF J. S. FREEMAN

BOOK TWO

CITIZEN

Yvonne Anderson

Citizen (The Four Lives of J. S. Freeman, #2)
ISBN 978-1-946985-10-1

This novel is a work of fiction. Characters, plot, and incidents are products of the author's imagination, and any similarity to people living or dead, whether on Earth or Umban, is coincidental.

TABLE OF CONTENTS

BOOK 2 – CITIZEN

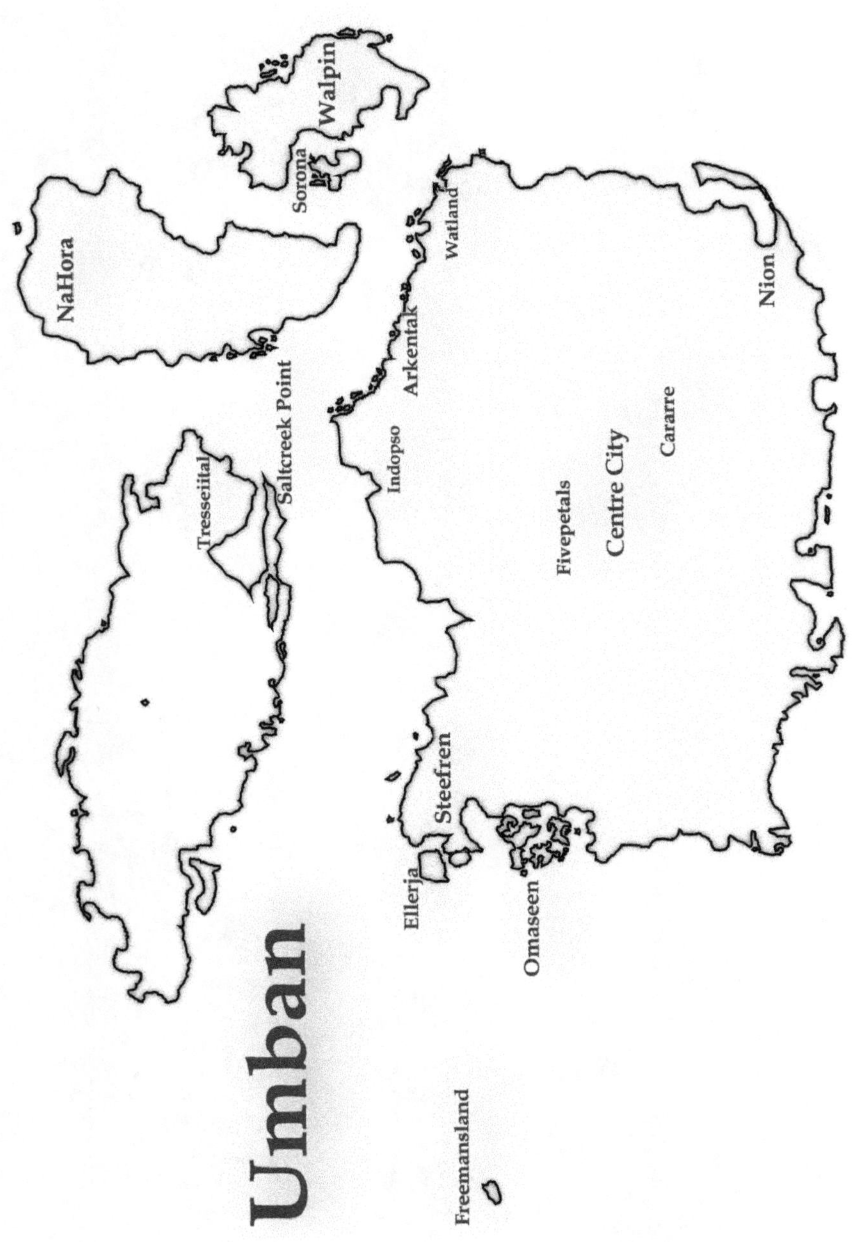
Walpin
Sorona
NaHora
Watland
Arkentak
Nion
Saltcreek Point
Indopso
Cararre
Fivepetals
Centre City
Tresseiital
Steefren
Ellerja
Omaseen
Umban
Freemansland

Here's a rough diagram of the island Freemansland, nicknamed The Land of Many Mysteries:

Some of this story takes place in a region of Umban called Arkentak. This might help you visualize it:

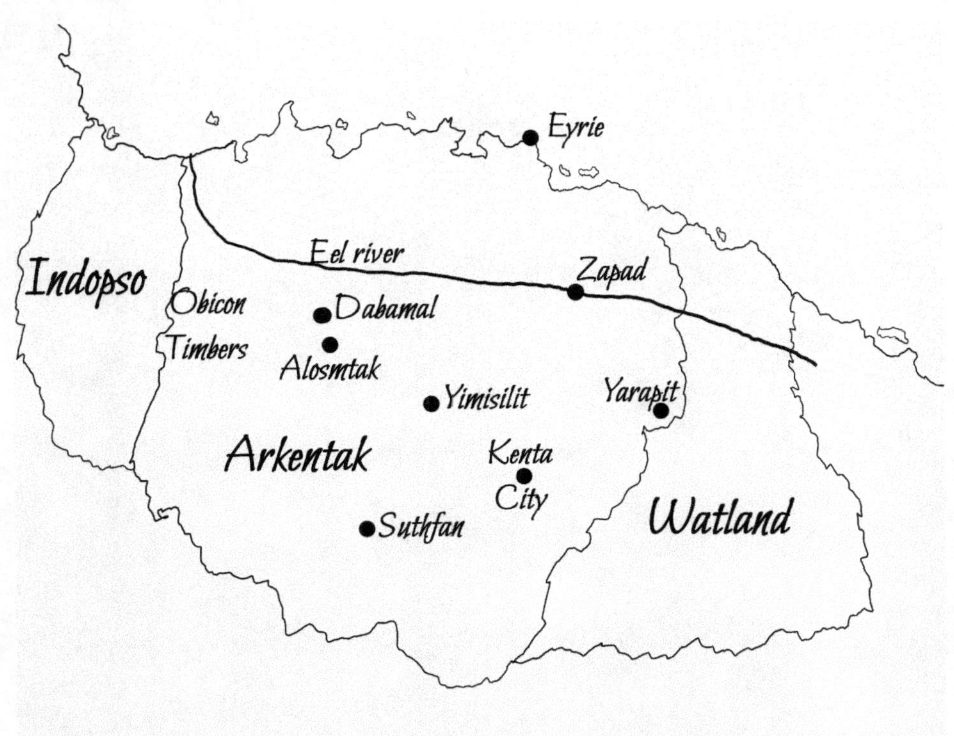

The Four Lives of J. S. Freeman
RECAP OF BOOK 1,
STILLWATERS

THE SERIES BEGINS with J. S. (Jemma) Freeman's first life:

Motherless from birth and rejected by her father, she's surviving as best she can on the island of Freemansland where she was born. Her one consolation is her twin brother, Jeriah, who watches out for her. Her greatest terror is her older brother, Ibro, who does bad things to little girls.

When Ibro catches her alone one evening, Jeriah comes to her rescue. In the melee, her father and Ibro both die. Now orphaned, Jemma and Jeriah are wards of the City—the powerful global entity that Jemma holds responsible for everything wrong with the world—and put in the care of an aunt they never knew they had. Thus begins Jemma's second life.

The City sends the twins to the Academy to get a modern education. They discover their old friend, Mayne Dabo, is also a student there. In order to keep the other boys from bothering Jemma, Mayne leads people to believe that he and Jemma have a marriage arrangement under an old and respected tradition on Freemansland.

Near the end of their time at the Academy, Mayne convinces Jemma and Jeriah to join the military after graduation. The recruiter promises they'll all three serve together, and if they enlist for ten years, they'll be granted citizenship upon their discharge.

The recruiter wasn't lying about the citizenship, but the three are sent to different branches of the military.

Being separated from her brother almost sends Jemma over the brink. It's surprising it doesn't, for in her first life, she became host to two stelli, parasitic worms that live in the brain. An infected person is called a stellasede.

As long as the worms are dormant, they do no harm; but when they become active, the stellasede goes mad and dies. Stressful situations are believed to cause the worms to awaken. Yet against the odds, Jemma survives the rigorous training and begins her military career in peak health.

Jeriah marries and starts a family, causing Jemma to feel separated from him by more than distance.

During this lonely time, Jemma has a professional relationship with Ashgrey (Grey) Standtall, a man of high pedigree. She despises all the highborn (Citizens First Class, or CFCs), and she privately refers to them as "pigeonheads" because their protruding brows remind her of the physician who treated her for her stelli, Dr. Pigeon.

Grey is a pigeonhead, and he is unaccountably attracted to Jemma despite her low-born status. Because of the abuse she suffered in childhood, however, she is mistrustful of men and doesn't wish to be attracted to anyone sexually. His proposal of marriage shocks her. Eventually she accepts, and they become officially betrothed.

Jemma has always considered the CFCs to be cruel and self-absorbed. But when Grey brings her home to meet his family, their kindness toward her and their honorable ways cause her to see she has misjudged them. This is especially a shock because, as a member of the Ruling Council, Grey's father should be among the worst of the villains.

Seeing the Standtalls' sterling character, she resolves to put her lawless Freemansland upbringing behind her and embrace this family's nobility as her own.

❧ Chapter 1 ❧

AND THEN THERE'S *MY* FAMILY

MY MEETING WITH Grey's family at the Standtall estate went far better than I had any right to expect. Only after I got home did it occur to me that turning my back on my Freemansland roots and becoming a Standtall might mean cutting myself off from my brother.

About a week after we returned, I had a video call with Jeriah. Grey and I sat side by side on the sofa in my apartment. When Jeriah's face came into view, his blue eyes lit on the pigeonhead beside me, and his expression hardened.

I spoke brightly. "Riah, hello! It's time you met my betrothed, Ashgrey Standtall."

All three of us were in uniform, and Jeriah stood, lifting the phone with him so we could see, and saluted. "Commander."

Grey had no choice but to return the salute, after which Riah sat back down. Then, as if as an afterthought, stood again and repeated the gesture. "My apologies, Information Officer Freeman. I should salute you, too."

I snapped, "Stop it, Riah. Don't be like this."

"Like what? Respectful of my superiors? Forgive me, please."

How could someone I loved so much infuriate me so? "We're family, you stu—" Oops. A Standtall would never call a person *stupid*, let alone the rest of what almost slipped from my lips. "And off duty. And six hundred kilometers apart. You don't have to salute your sister in these circumstances. What the glish."

Though Grey tensed as if sensing danger, his speech was civil, if a bit too formal. "Your sister speaks of you often, Jeriah. You are very important to her, and I am anxious to meet you personally. Until that can be arranged, however, I suppose a video call will have to do."

Riah eyed him warily. "Yes, sir, it will do."

I had to get a real conversation going, and soon. But what did these two have in common? Me. That was about it. "You love me, Riah, don't you?"

He pursed his lips and looked down briefly before turning his blues back up to mine. "More than anything."

"I know you do." I wrapped my arm around Grey's. "And so does he. He'll never hurt me, because he loves me. But if you reject the man I love, *you'll* hurt me. Don't do that, Ri."

Grey let out a pent-up breath. "She's a wise woman, your sister. Look, I know how you feel about us pigeonheads—"

Riah gave a little start at hearing the word.

"Yes, she told me about Dr. Pigeon and the name you call people with—" he ran a finger along his brow "—certain cranial characteristics. But I'm not Dr. Pigeon. I hope—and your sister is confident—that you'll come to accept me for who I am, as she does."

Riah's gaze went back and forth between Grey and me as Grey continued, "And who I am is someone who happens to love your sister more than life itself."

When Riah looked dubious, I spoke up. "What? You think no one could love me?"

I knew what he was thinking, because our thoughts often connected. *Mayne loves you.* But what he said was, "No, I don't think that."

"You just never figured I'd fall for someone who's City." The rest of the term, *slime*, went unsaid.

Riah nodded. "Yeah, well, I can see this is the way it's going to be. So, okay, I'll try to live with it." He glanced at Grey. "No offense, Commander."

Grey nodded. "None taken. But we're family now, and my family calls me by my first name."

Riah leaned back in his chair. "Right. So, Jem, you went to meet this new family of yours a couple weeks ago. Tell me about them." No one could call his manner gracious, but at least he wasn't hanging up on me as I'd feared.

I launched into a discussion of the people I'd met when visiting Sentinel Pines. I made it a point to bring Grey into the conversation as much as possible, asking him to fill in some of the details.

Riah listened with little comment for several minutes, but his expression and body language said he wasn't impressed.

"Oh, you might find this interesting." I grasped for something to melt his icy stare. "The kids loved it when I told them stories. They couldn't get enough of them."

His brows lifted. "Do tell."

"Yeah, it surprised me, too. At first, the kids terrified me, honestly, 'cause you know I'm not comfortable with kids. They're like alien creatures. But the first night, when their parents told them it was time to get ready for bed, Grey's oldest niece, Willow—she's his sister Silver's daughter. She asked me if I could tell them a bedtime story. And Grey, here, comes out with, 'Aunt Jem's a good storyteller.' I don't know where that came from, but—"

Grey graced me with a smile of adoration. "Because you are. You have a way with words."

"Well, I never thought I did." I shrugged. "But they persuaded me to come up with something, so I told them that old story about the baby dragon wandering on the sharpfall who came upon some swamp bears."

Jeriah nodded. "Little Goldenscale."

"Yeah. Except I changed the story so it wasn't a dragon, it was a little girl. And I made the swamp bears out to be bumbling idiots. I guess it wasn't really the Little Goldenscale story, but that was the inspiration."

Grey broke in. "She did a brilliant job. I can't believe it was off the cuff, because it sounded well rehearsed. Not just the kids, but all the adults were drawn into the tale. Unfortunately, the kids weren't sleepy afterward. They clamored for more."

I chuckled. "I'm glad their parents said no, because I don't know what I'd have told them next."

"But she was ready the next night when they asked her again." Gray put his arm around me. "She's now the official storyteller of the family. Everybody loves to hear her Freemansland tales."

Jeriah grunted. "So you tell bedtime stories to *his* nieces and nephews, but you've never even met your own?"

Grey turned to me, his face asking wordless questions.

I flushed. "You know I love your kids, Riah. I've just never had the opportunity to—"

"That's a steaming pile of honey."

I know that doesn't sound vile, but on Freemansland, it's a term almost as foul as Cityslime. *Honeypot* was what we called the hole where you relieved yourself, so you can guess what *honey* referred to.

Jeriah glared. "Your namesake is three years old, and you've never made an effort to meet her. Or her brother. You've never even talked about it."

I was about to object, but he plowed on. "Have you called Seena lately?"

My mind grappled with what sounded like a change in subject. "What?"

"Have you bothered to call her, see how she's doing, talk to the kids?"

"Well, no, but—"

"Slime, you never even ask me about them. Every time we talk anymore, it's always about you, you, you. You and your beloved Grey, your wedding plans, your this and your that. Sounds to me like—"

Grey raised his hand. "Hold on a minute, Jeriah." He turned to me. "What is he saying, Freeman? Is it true? You've never met your own niece and nephew?"

I felt short of breath. "I haven't, but like I said—"

"That's going to change." Grey addressed Jeriah. "I'm sorry, I had no idea. I'll see what I can do to get you all together just as soon as—"

Jeriah interrupted. "Thank you, Commander, but don't bother. It seems she has a new family now and doesn't need mine. It was nice meeting you, sir."

The screen went blank.

I wanted to grab the device and throw it across the room, but that's not the sort of thing a Standtall would do.

Instead, I huffed with indignation. "Well, that was rude. I can't believe he hung up on us."

I had every intention of getting up and putting some distance between myself and Grey, who radiated disapproval in waves that threatened to overwhelm me. But he grabbed my hand and pulled me back when I tried to rise.

"Hold on a minute."

I tried to pull away, but he held firm. "What was he talking about? Why have you never visited them?"

His grip was more pushy than painful, but I didn't like his tone. Even worse, I disliked the way he thought he could tell me how to run my life. What business was it of his that I'd never found the courage to see Jeriah's kids? I was good to Grey's family, wasn't I? Wasn't that all that mattered?

I looked down at his hand holding mine. "You're hurting me," I lied.

He let go. "I'm sorry, I didn't mean to."

I hopped up and fled to the bedroom.

He rose too, but I was quicker. His call of "Freeman!" vied for last-word status with the slam of my door.

I didn't answer him. How could I explain what I didn't understand myself?

⁂

ABOUT THAT "YOU'RE hurting me" lie? Greater import lay behind those words than you might think.

Shortly before we left Sentinel Pines, Grey's mother had one final meeting with me. His father was away on business, so it was "just us two girls," as she put it. It was an intimacy I never thought I'd share with someone of her class, but her warmth put me completely at ease.

She started off talking about the wedding, probing considerately to avoid stepping on the toes of anyone in my family who expected to help with the arrangements.

"I've never been to a wedding," I confessed, much to her astonishment. Once I managed to convince her that was true, I told her, "I have no idea what a wedding should be like. The thought of planning something like that is almost enough to make me break out in a rash."

She laughed. Apparently that phrase wasn't such a well-worn cliché in her world as it was in mine. "Oh, Jemma dear, we cannot have you itching on your wedding day. Are you sure you don't have someone in the family to help you? Your aunt? One of your cousins is about your age, I believe?"

I shook my head. "People get married on Freemansland, but they don't make a big deal about it. You should be the one to help me, since you know how these things work."

She took a little convincing, but eventually I got it across to her that I truly wanted her to take charge.

"It is such a shame you'll be so far away. But, no matter. I shall meet with Zeffa. She is the wedding planner Silver used, and she does a marvelous job. We will get some ideas together, and then I shall run them by you to see what you think."

I wanted to say, *I'd rather you kept me out of it. Just tell me what to do.* But I was afraid she'd have a stroke. "That sounds perfect. Thank you so much for taking care of it for me. I can't tell you what a relief it is to know it's in such good hands."

Every breath of that was true, believe me.

After a little more chatter on that subject, she turned to a topic that caught me completely off guard. "We have not discussed this before, Jemma dear, but before we go any farther with the wedding plans, I should tell you about the agreement Mr. Standtall and I will require that you sign."

My heart seized up and my stomach turned a somersault. "Ma'am?" It had something to do with having children, didn't it? I just knew something like this would happen. I'd already agreed to have their doctors look into my fertility issues. What more could they ask?

She must have noticed my stricken look, because she reached out and took my hand. "You have nothing to fear. The matter is serious, but the agreement will be for your protection."

"I don't understand."

"I can see that you do not. And why would you?" She patted my hand. "It is an unusual request."

She scooted closer so she could put her arm around me. "I already love you like a daughter. You are safe here. I hope you know that."

I nodded and swallowed again. "You've made me feel very welcome."

She hugged me. "I am so glad you feel that way. Mr. Standtall and I are so pleased that Ashgrey has chosen you. We could have found no better match for him had we searched the world for one." She gave a chuckle. "Truth be told, we did just that. Or at least, we tried, until he asked us to kindly cease and desist."

I could imagine that conversation and smiled at the thought.

"He is a man of discerning tastes, to be sure." She removed her arm from my shoulders but held my hand. "He is, however, an exacting man, as are all the Standtalls. Though he controls his temper well, he does have one. That, too, is typical. Traditionally, the men in our family—not just our family, but many of the City Fathers—have been known to be, shall we say, hard on their wives."

Where in the world was she going with this? Weren't all men like that?

"In the past, they often took pride in the extent to which they kept their wives under subjection. Even today, some men in our class think nothing of mistreating their women."

I failed to see how that separated them from anyone else. She seemed to expect a response from me, though, so for lack of anything else to say, I nodded. "I see."

"Ashgrey's great-grandfather and his brothers decided it was time to put a stop to that, and they vowed formally to never strike their wives. Since that time, anyone marrying into the family is required to sign a solemn agreement that neither husband nor wife will strike the other. The woman must promise that if her husband breaks his vow, she will leave him. Immediately. She must never let it happen again. If her own family cannot or will not take her in and she has no means to fend for herself, the Standtalls will protect and support her. We will not allow any woman in our family to go through what so many have endured, and continue to be put through even today. It simply will not happen in a Standtall household."

I found my tongue. "I have never heard of such a thing."

"Oh, yes, I regret that it is true. The things some men do to their women should not be spoken of."

"No, that's not what I mean. I'm aware domestic violence is widespread. What I've never heard of is a family providing protection like this. I'm— I'm floored, quite frankly."

She patted my hand. "We have raised both our boys properly. I cannot believe you would be in any danger even without the agreement. But we are committed to this."

"Though I can't imagine Ashgrey ever striking me, I'll certainly sign the pledge, if you require it."

The contract would be signed on the wedding day, so it wasn't yet in effect. But when I accused Grey of hurting me, he took the charge seriously. In fact, he dropped my hand as if it burned him.

Once I was safe in my room, I reflected on how a woman might manipulate a man with that mindset.

Then my conscience, recently sensitized by my association with the virtuous Standtalls, reared an angry head and glared at my heart. How could I think such a thing?

He tapped on the door. "Freeman?"

I couldn't endure his goodness. His righteousness was an assault to my shriveled, warped character. "I think you should go home. I'm not feeling well."

"Well, of course not." I heard no trace of sympathy in his tone. "You should be sick over this. Why have you never made an effort to see your brother's family?"

What business was that of his? I'd visit Jeriah's kids when I was good and ready.

"Freeman." It was a command, not a question. Maybe he wouldn't be so easy to manipulate.

But did I really want a man who was? "Go away."

"I know you're not sick. You just don't want to talk about it." He sounded almost perturbed enough to barge in without an invitation.

"Go away." I watched the door, poised for action should I see the slightest movement—though I had no idea what action I would take.

Nothing happened for a long, tense half-minute. When he spoke, it was not reassuring. "I'm going. But don't think for a minute you're getting out of this. We will straighten this out, and soon."

I stared at the door, listening to the retreat of his heavy footsteps, the opening and closing of my apartment's entrance. Only after I could hear him no more did I let out my breath.

The image of Jeriah's furrowed brow danced across my vision, and his words taunted me. *Your namesake is three years old, and you've never made an effort to meet her.*

Grey's face took the place of Jeriah's. *What is he saying, Jemma. Is that true?* And then his stern, *We will straighten this out, and soon.*

Jeriah was right. I had been deliberately avoiding Seena and the kids. But it wasn't my fault it hurt so much to see them.

And Grey was right too. I should be ashamed. The fact that I wasn't sick over it was itself a condemnation.

Both Jeriah and Grey were so much better than me. But they both loved me. How could they?

What would a Standtall do?

To begin with, if I were a Standtall, I wouldn't hide like this. When a Standtall committed a wrong, he confessed it. He made it right.

My legs turned to gel eels, and I collapsed onto the bed. I hadn't the first idea how to apologize, mostly because I'd always convinced myself I never had anything to apologize for.

But I was wrong now, and sooner or later, I'd have to admit it. I couldn't hide in the bedroom forever.

I tried to envision facing Grey and confessing the truth. It *was* my choice to not see my niece and nephew. I'd had ample opportunity, but always found an excuse not to. What would he do when I told him?

Make me admit it to Jeriah, for starters. And make me remedy the situation.

Confound those Standtalls and their slithering, slotting nobility.

✤ Chapter 2 ✤

I STAND TALL UNDER PRESSURE

THAT NIGHT, THE battle in my mind kept me awake for hours. But that was only one small strife in the world.

Unbeknownst to me, while I lay sleepless, Kentan rebels destroyed the grids supplying power to lower-income areas of several towns across Arkentak.

Why would they do that to their own people, you might ask? Good question, and the answer is ugly: so they could then plant rumors that the City had cut off the power as punishment for recent acts of violence.

The City didn't work that way, but the people believed what the prophets of the High Priestess told them: the City hated Our Lady and her Kentan children and would never let them prosper. Subsequently, when City-owned utility crews appeared to make repairs and restore power, angry mobs attacked. Troops called in to protect them were baited, tricking them into retaliating against parties who were uninvolved. Though all this caused harm to numerous Kentans, it served the rebels' purpose of fueling the growing anti-City sentiment.

Then hackers infiltrated what we thought were secure networks. The location of our secret headquarters in Dabamal was compromised, and we were forced to move our facilities. Until the phone systems were secured, we had to resort to the most primitive means of communicating.

All this happened with breathtaking speed. It was obvious the people behind the rebellion were not only creative thinkers but had allies in many quarters. Everyone in the Division put in very long hours.

The rift between Riah and me lay like a seeping wound. I mostly ignored the pain, allowing my work to absorb my attention. But when my mind wandered back to Jeriah's hurt accusations—and worse yet, the grave disappointment in Grey's dark eyes—an ache rose within me.

Yes, we really did need to fix this. But I didn't know how. And too many other things needed fixing first.

GREY HAD BEEN away for two weeks dealing with Division emergencies in various parts of Arkentak. Since the night I'd retreated to my bedroom and left him and his heavy brows on the other side of the door, our infrequent communications had been brief and businesslike, with the occasional endearing utterance thrown in to reassure one another.

But now, late in the day, he appeared at my makeshift office in the corner of an ancient cellar. The new HQ wasn't a wine cellar, but I did have a bottle of whisky tucked in a desk drawer, and I periodically took a sip to keep me going. I'd just closed the drawer when Grey came in and loomed in front of me.

My heart lurched. Was it delight at seeing him, or guilt at having been drinking on the job? Alcohol wasn't strictly forbidden, but Grey seemed to think I imbibed too much, and I couldn't deal with another layer of his disapproval.

I popped a mint into my mouth and offered him one. "Hey. Need a pick-me-up?"

"We all do. Thanks." He took a mint, then tossed a glance at the other people in the area and apparently decided to forego a kiss.

Considering my boozy breath, I didn't mind.

He dropped a folder on my desk. "Here."

"What's this?" I opened the file. It held travel orders. I looked up at him, brows raised.

"I've finally had a chance to address, ah, that matter we discussed a while back. About your neglect of your family."

I stared at the orders. "What neglect? I told you, I simply haven't had—"

"You haven't had the opportunity to see them. So you said. Well, I'm giving you one. It took some doing, but I've arranged for both you and Jeriah to go to Saltcreek Point. Though you'll be on different assignments, you'll have time to get together with him. At his home. Meet his children, for crying cornballs."

I sat back in my chair and frowned up at him. "You can't do that. This is between him and me."

He laid his big hands on my desk and leaned toward me, his voice low but tone firm. "The arrangements are made. You are doing this."

If I answered with his face so close, he'd smell my breath. So I wrinkled my nose, covered my mouth and nose with one hand, and waved the other between us. "Whew! What have you been eating?"

He stood upright. "A mint. But I might ask you the same thing."

Avoiding his sharp gaze, I reviewed the orders. "So we're leaving in the morning?"

"*You're* leaving in the morning. You two will find it easier to iron out your differences without me around."

"You're right about that. But I wish you could go. Seems like a lifetime since we've been together." I ventured a plaintive look his direction.

"I know." His expression had softened. "But in a little over two months, we'll be married. Then we can be together forever."

LOVE DOES STRANGE things to a person.

At first, I was angry. How dare he? Being a Citizen First Class didn't give him the right to dictate how the rest of us lived.

But then the "together forever" rolled over me, and I realized he was seeing the big picture here. If we were to be happy together, I'd have to make things right with Jeriah. Facilitating that was thoughtful. My resentment turned to gratitude.

But when I saw how much work these new orders created, my warm fuzzies grew spines and claws.

The official purpose for my visit—and Grey couldn't have sent me away at a time like this without one—was to deliver a presentation to a gathering of bigwigs on the situation in Arkentak. It was to cover the weaknesses the Kentans had exploited, how we had responded, and the steps we were taking to get on top of things.

Grey had provided a general outline of what was to be covered but left it up to me to flesh it out. "Ordinarily, this would be the responsibility of a higher ranking officer," he'd said. "But the truth is, personal bias aside, you're the best I've got for this sort of thing. You know how to convey information in an organized manner without putting people to sleep. If anyone can get the brass to see what's going on here, you can."

Remembering those words renewed some of my warmth for him.

But it was a big job, and I already had a great deal to accomplish before I left. As a result, I never had a chance to close my eyes before leaving for the airport in the morning.

Waiting to board, I called Grey. "I hope you realize I've been up all night, thanks to you." My feelings at that moment were pure irritation.

"You're welcome. But you'll have a chance to get some sleep on the flight."

I yawned. "I think I'll do that. Does Riah know I'm coming?"

"Not unless you told him."

No, of course Grey wouldn't have contacted him. What was I thinking? "I'll give him a call." I looked up at the sound of the boarding call. "I've got to go."

"So do I. But listen. Your presentation is important. If you come across as weary, that's okay. We're all stretched thin here, and they need to know that. Just don't come across as— I mean, make sure you get the situation across to them."

I narrowed my eyes. "Were you going to say *don't come across as incompetent?*"

"If I had any concerns as to your ability, I wouldn't be sending you. But they're calling your flight. Give my love to your niece and nephew."

I scowled as I disconnected the call, snatched my bag, and strode to the boarding queue. Under the cuff of my left sleeve, my betrothal bracelet scraped against my skin. The reminder of its presence usually evoked a satisfied smile, but not so much now.

Was Jeriah right? Was this whole thing with Grey a colossal, pigeonheaded mistake?

I pulled out my phone and softly dictated Jeriah a text. "Ordered to a meeting at the Point. Can I stop by your place tonight?"

The answer didn't come until I was in the air and sleeping soundly. Snoring, I guessed, from the dry, raspy feeling in my throat. The phone's vibration made me jump, and it took several seconds to orient myself.

The text was brief. "Who arranged this?"

My mind struggled. Who arranged what? The message was from Jeriah. What was he talking about?

Oh. Of course. He'd been ordered to the Point too. Until my message, he'd been expecting a nice reunion with Seena and kids. The timing of my sudden self-invitation was, in fact, suspicious.

I answered. "Who do you think?" Then as an afterthought, I sent a second reply. "Commander sent me to a meeting at the Point. Seeing you is my doing."

A few minutes later he responded. "Come alone."

"Just me. Lemme know what time's best." I sent the text and slipped back into sleep with the phone on my lap.

I awoke about a half hour before we landed, which gave me time to get my mind in gear. On the ground, I freshened up in the restroom while mentally reviewing my presentation.

Some time later, I entered the meeting room, fully prepared to speak. But not to face such an audience. Grey hadn't told me I'd be giving this talk before the Chief Commanders of all the military branches as well as a number of City Cabinet ministers. One of them, the Minister of Domestic Peace, I'd met before: Stal Standtall, my soon-to-be father-in-law.

At the sight of all those heavily-medaled uniforms and heavy-browed faces, my heart raced. But when I took a slow, deep breath, I realized Grey had judged me worthy to tell them what they needed to hear. If he thought so, it might be true. I would live up this his trust.

With the betrothal bracelet beneath my cuff pressing against my wrist, I gave my data stick to the media projectionist and waited to be introduced. I was ready for this. I was ready to stand tall.

Minister Standtall was in charge of the assembly. That made sense, since he was in charge of keeping domestic peace. He called the meeting to order, said some preliminary things I only half-listened to because they didn't apply to me, and then introduced me as "a representative of our people on the front lines" who had been summoned to give an overview of the situation. He never mentioned our relationship, and as I rose, I didn't either.

My voice was steady and my hands not the least bit shaky as I came to the podium. "Thank you, Minister." I surveyed my frowning audience. "Gentlemen, ladies. Thank you for your interest in what's going on in Arkentak. I have a good deal to cover, but I'll try not to take too much of your valuable time." And with every bit of professionalism I could muster, made my presentation to a mostly bored-looking room.

That was one thing Grey had warned me about. Most of these people didn't think they had any business being there. Each had his or her own area or department to oversee, and they were all doing their jobs. If the people in charge of keeping the peace in Arkentak weren't doing theirs, why was that their concern?

It was my purpose to show that it was everyone's concern. Arkentak didn't exist in a bubble, but was connected on many levels to the rest of the world. What began in Arkentak would reverberate through all those connections and shake the whole globe.

I was thankful for my mind-sharpening stellas juice that day. I gave the presentation perfectly, watching as if from outside my body. How had I known to say that? What had inspired me to insert that image there? What genius had led me to make that point from such a clever angle? I honestly didn't remember coming up with this stuff, but there it was, pouring out of my mouth with a knowledge and competence that amazed no one more than me.

And then it was over.

I looked out across my audience, every member of which looked riveted. Thoughtful. Disturbed. I glanced at Minister Standtall. "I would be happy to take questions, if we have time."

He gave a sober nod.

"We do? Very well. I'm not, of course, privy to every detail, but if anyone would like clarification of what I've touched on, I'll answer what questions I can."

No one spoke for several moments. I wished Minister Standtall would dismiss me, but he remained seated, and I avoided looking his way. Then a woman raised her hand. I recognized her as Land Forces General Rheta Denn, reputed to be a woman of no mercy. Her hard expression did nothing to belie those rumors.

I nodded to her. "General Denn, ma'am? How might I help you?"

"You say you're not privy to every detail. Why would the Division send a First Information Officer to this meeting? Why not someone who knows something?"

"I don't question my orders, ma'am. I merely obey them."

Small smiles flickered across a couple of faces.

General Denn didn't smile. "Your name again, Information Officer?"

"Freeman, ma'am. First Information Officer Jemima Freeman."

She scowled. "You're the one who brought down Colonel Redruff, aren't you?"

I tried to maintain my composure, but the accusation took me by surprise, and my expression may have shown it. "With all due respect, General, no. I'm sorry to say Colonel Redruff unraveled his own career."

Another general rose and faced Denn. The patch on his sleeve said he was Chief of the IA Division, Fad Pymon. "IO Freeman is right about that, Rheta, and we all know it." He turned and addressed the room. "And I believe she's right about the rest of it as well. Instead of attacking the messenger, each of us needs to go home and clean house. I expect we all have a little dirt under our rugs here and there." He gave me a good-natured once-over. "Have you found anything rotten in the back of my closet, Freeman?"

"I've never looked in your closet, sir. I only go where I'm sent."

"Well, then, I'm sending you. If there are any rebel sympathizers in my Division, I want to know about it. I'll get in touch with your commander tomorrow to make it happen."

Would I be leaving Arkentak? And Grey? I hoped not, but I wasn't lying when I said I didn't question orders. "As you wish, General Pymon."

Minister Standtall chose that moment to rise. "I won't contradict you, Pymon. A thorough housecleaning is definitely called for, but we should be methodical about this. Let's discuss the best course of action before we jump into anything."

He turned to me. "IO Freeman, thank you for coming. You have provided us with invaluable information, and we will most certainly act upon it. May we keep the data stick?"

"Of course, Minister." I addressed the room with a salute. "Sirs, ma'ams. Thank you." I made for the door, which a Ministry Security man opened, and I exited.

It wasn't until I'd traversed the building all the way back to the foyer that my knees started to tremble. I sank into the nearest chair to gather my strength.

A guard hastened toward me. "Excuse me, ma'am. Your badge?"

I looked up at him blankly. "Pardon me?"

"Your Visitor's badge, ma'am. You forgot to return it."

"Oh, yes. Of course." I unclipped it from my jacket. "Thank you for reminding me." To disguise the trembling of my hand as I passed him the badge, I faked a cough, burying my mouth in the crook of my elbow. "Excuse me."

"Can I get you anything, ma'am? A water, perhaps?"

I shook my head. "No, thank you." I wanted to rest a little longer, but not there. "I'll be on my way now." I stood and headed for the door.

The presentation had gone well, of that I was sure. What happened next was out of my hands.

What happened next for me, was meeting my niece and nephew.

❧ Chapter 3 ❧

———

MEET THE FAMILY (PART II)

———

RIAH AND SEENA'S tidy little rental house stood shoulder-to-shoulder with a row of similar units. Colorful. Clean. Lots of pavement and not much grass, but a few trees stood here and there, especially around the playground at the end of the row. The neighborhood was part of the affordable housing the City made available to military families at Saltcreek Point, and it was surprisingly pleasant.

I rang the buzzer for Unit 8, and a moment later, Riah opened the bright orange door.

His blue eyes shone beneath smooth, non-jutting brows, and his finely etched lips tilted in a crooked smile. "Come on in."

I felt my own half-smile form. "Thanks." I stepped in. "I'm glad you agreed to see me. I could scarcely blame you if you didn't."

"Hey." He took me in his arms. "Whatever else you may be, you're still my sister."

I hugged him back. Hard. "Call me whatever you want. I won't deny it."

Seena's voice came from my left. "No one can deny you're brother and sister. You look almost exactly alike. Glish, but you're beautiful."

I released Riah and turned to grab Seena in an even more enthusiastic embrace. "I can't believe I waited this long. I haven't seen you since the academy, and here you've been my sister-in-law for what, five years now?"

"Six," Riah said.

"Yes, six." Seena sounded breathless. "You're crushing me."

I let go. "Oh, sorry! I'm just so glad to see you!" I hugged her again, but not so hard.

I'm ashamed to say it, but the reason I hugged her again was only partly because I was glad to see her. Mostly, I didn't want to have to look at her, for her appearance jarred me. She wore no makeup, her hair was scraggly, her clothes frumpy, and—well, let's just say there was a lot to hug. She seemed a sad mismatch for the dashing Riah, but they were happy together, so who was I to judge?

I sniffed the air. "You didn't hold dinner for me, did you?"

Seena grinned. "No, we ate, but we saved you something."

I sniffed again. "Bicio blossoms? Are you kidding? Where did you find those around here?"

"You can get anything at the international market. People from everywhere are stationed at the Point, and the City ships in produce from all over the world. If you were going to be here longer, I'd take you to check it out."

Seena's round face beamed. She always loved cooking, which was why she went into food services after graduating from the Academy. But I couldn't share her enthusiasm. "I'm afraid I wouldn't appreciate it. I don't cook. At all."

Seena stared at me like I'd lost my mind, but Jeriah looked amused. "Does your pigeonhead know that?"

I pretended the remark didn't annoy me. "So where are those kids of yours? You hiding them from me?"

Seena smiled. "They're in the bedroom."

Jeriah was already on his way, and I followed.

The house was clean, orderly, and in good repair, but small. In about four strides we were in the kids' room. Two beds wouldn't have fit in the tiny space, but this was a Freeman home—the kids slept on mats, which were now rolled up and placed on a shelf.

Little Kyee Jem shrieked, "Daddy!" But when she saw me, she stopped in mid-scamper to stare, her blue eyes widening in a fresh-as-dawn, round-cheeked face.

He picked her up. "Hey, KJ. This is your Auntie Jem."

She pressed herself against him and watched me from behind a veil of soft brown hair.

Meanwhile, I'd moved out of the doorway so Seena could go in, and she lifted the baby from where he sat on the floor. He'd been mouthing a toy when we came in—a puffy, soft plastic dragon—and now he tapped her on the head with it.

Seena held his hand still and directed his attention my way. "Jeo, say hello to Auntie Jem."

Riah spoke to his daughter in the odd, high voice adults use with small children. "Want to go see your auntie? She's Daddy's twin sister, did you know that? Want to go see her?"

He shifted her as if to pass her to me, and she let out a shriek. "No!"

Then Jeo joined in, and in about six seconds, I had a headache.

A SHORT TIME LATER, the five of us sat around a table made for four in a room the size of the bathtub in the guest suite at Sentinel Pines. Cozy.

After the kids' eruption, Seena had taken them into the kitchen with the promise of a snack, and they lost interest in me. Riah and I stayed behind to pick up toys and lay out the bed mats. When he got out their nightclothes, I marveled that a human could fit into such tiny things.

Contrasting these kids' childhood with my own, I thought aloud, "You're a better father than ours was."

He grunted. "Seena keeps me civilized."

"I'm told a good wife is the greatest of blessings." I watched him pull down the window shade. "My future father-in-law told me that. And he's a wise man."

Riah shrugged. "He's right in Seena's case, anyway. Ready for some of those bicio blossoms?"

"In a minute. First, I want to tell you—" I ahem'ed away the gravel that suddenly appeared in my throat. "I was jealous of you."

"What?"

"That's why I was reluctant to visit. I couldn't stand it that you and Seena had a family, and I had nothing and nobody. And even though I have someone now, I'll still never have any children. I guess I sorta thought that if I never actually met yours, they wouldn't be real to me, and that would make it easier to deal with."

The tender look on Riah's face almost brought me to tears. He wrapped me in his arms. "I'm sorry. I had no idea you felt that way."

"You have nothing to apologize for. I do. And speaking of civilizing influences, Grey is that to me. I never would have come if he hadn't insisted on it." I relaxed in my brother's embrace. "You can't imagine how glad I am he did."

Riah released me. "Yeah. Me too. Your marrying a Cityslime still scares me. But I have to admit the new Jem is an improvement. If he's responsible for the change, I'll shut up about it." His crooked smile made a mischievous appearance. "For now, anyway."

"I guess that's all I can ask for."

He gestured toward the door. "Let's go get those blossoms."

Even reheated, the greasy things were delicious, especially when dipped in the sauce Seena had made. When I offered to share mine with KJ, she actually sat in my lap. After the blossoms were gone and she'd licked the sauce bowl clean, she examined the buttons and insignia patches on my uniform. Then she discovered my betrothal bracelet, which she declared to be "weawy pwetty."

"She means *really pretty*," Seena translated, adding, "We're looking into the possibility of speech thewapy."

Riah shook his head. "She's only three. She'll come around."

Seena's expression told me they'd discussed this before, but she apparently chose not to argue in front of me.

We sat and talked, letting the kids entertain us until Seena told them it was bedtime.

Jeriah stood and lifted KJ from my lap. "Want Auntie Jem to tell you a bedtime story? I hear she's good at it."

She bobbed her head, so I waited on her mat in the bedroom while their parents got them ready. Then Riah sat on the other end of the mat, Seena nursed Jeo in the rocking chair, and KJ curled up between Riah and me.

"Did Mommy or Daddy ever tell you about the stillwater and the sharpfalls on Freemansland?"

KJ shook her head. "What'th thtillwatehs an' shopfaws?"

Speech therapy might not be a bad idea. "Since you live on the Point, I imagine you've seen the ocean, haven't you?"

She nodded and stuck her thumb in her mouth.

"A stillwater is a big body of water like an ocean, but there's no current, no big waves. That's why they call it *still* water. It lies still, like you do when you're sleeping."

Seena broke in. "Take your thumb out of your mouth, Kyee Jem. You're not a baby." When KJ ignored her, Seena said, "Riah, take her thumb out of her mouth, would you?"

"She's a little kid, Seen. She's okay."

Seena made sound of exasperation. "I don't let her do that when *you're* not here."

Riah bent and rubbed foreheads with KJ. "But I'm here tonight, aren't I, baby girl? So if you want to thuck yo wittle thumb, you go wight ahead."

KJ somehow managed to grin and suck harder at the same time, while Seena rolled her eyes.

Remembering the time she'd taken a knife to the rat in Yarapit, I grew uncomfortable. "Maybe I should go. You don't get to see one another very often, and I don't want to be in the way."

I began to rise, but KJ bolted up, wide-eyed. "No!"

At the same time, Riah reached out and grabbed my arm. "Tell your story. KJ, you lie back down. I want to see you sleeping in the next two minutes." He held up four fingers. "Two minutes, do you hear?"

She giggled. "That's fouw fingewth, Daddy."

"You're right!" He looked at his hand in surprise. "Okay, then, four minutes. Do you hear me? I want you sound asleep in four minutes."

She giggled again, turned on her side, and popped her thumb in her mouth. "Okay, Auntie Jem. Tell me the thtowy."

Seena sighed. "She'd talk a lot better without that thumb—"

"Yes, Mama," Riah said. "Tell your story, Auntie Jem."

I spoke softly and slowly about a little girl sitting on a rock at the edge of the quiet waters. The gentle moon looked down to see its reflection, and it made a glow across the water in a long, soft stripe. A night gull flew over and cast a shadow, making it look like the moon's reflection winked at the girl. She winked back. A school of risingfish broke through the surface to snatch low-flying insects, slapping the water with their tails as they re-entered the stillwater. The little girl stood. "They're applauding for me." She bowed left and right. When a cloud passed over the moon, she said, "The moon's going to sleep." So she lay down on the soft mossy rock, stuck her thumb in her mouth, and went to sleep too.

Riah gently pulled the sleeping KJ's thumb from her mouth, Seena eased Jeo from her arms to his mat, and we tiptoed out, leaving the children to their slumbers.

I RETURNED TO Damabal late the next day. Before reporting to my own station at Royal Fern, I went to the Pea Vine Street location where Grey had his office.

When I reached his corner of the building, his door was closed. The muffled voices coming from inside did not sound happy. I tried not to pay attention to the words, but it was apparent that Grey was taking someone to task.

No one was around except Third Information Officer Diamel, who seemed absorbed in something on his computer.

I stopped at his desk and nodded toward the closed door. "The commander's in a meeting, I take it?"

Diamel blinked then removed his reading glasses. "You might say that. Hi, Freeman. I don't figure he'll be long, if you want to wait."

"I'll do that, if I may."

"If I let you leave without seeing him, it'll be me standing in there with my ears melting."

The voice on the other side of the door—the one that wasn't Grey's—sounded like he was arguing. I winced. Not a wise move on that guy's part.

Diamel chuckled. "Yeah, like I said. Wait for him. Please."

I found a chair nearby. "Rough day, huh?"

"Day, week, and month. One runs into another. How was the Point?"

"Like a world removed. Most people have no idea what's going on here, and most of those who do would rather not get involved.

They'll let us deal with it however we can, just so we keep the blood from splattering them."

He nodded. "How'd the presentation go?"

"It's in my report."

The commander's door opened then, and I stood and turned to look at a notice on the wall. I wanted to give the victim of Grey's wrath a chance to think he might slink out unseen. I did see him out of the corner of my eye, though, and recognized Spen, a fellow Specialist-now-First Information Officer with whom I'd worked in the past.

He looks a bit ashy and gray himself. I took no pleasure in his pain. I always liked Spen.

Daimel went to the doorway. "Commander? IO Freeman is here to see you."

"Send her in."

I didn't wait for him to relay the information. As soon as Daimel left the doorway, I was through it.

Grey rose from his desk. "What are you doing here?"

"Don't worry, I'm on my way to Royal Fern, and I'll make my report through the proper channels. But I wanted to stop here first to tell you something."

He extended his big hand as if expecting me to give him something.

I looked up at him. "What?"

He wiggled his fingers. "These are the proper channels. I sent you on the assignment, so you can make your report to me."

"Oh. Okay." I pulled from my pocket the encrypted data stick holding my report and placed it in his hand.

He set it on his desk, then turned back to me. "I got a call from my dad last night, so I know the presentation went well. But how about your meeting with your brother?"

I wanted to know what his father had said about me—wanted to know pretty intensely, in fact—but it took second place to my desire to give Grey the message I'd come here to deliver. "My meeting with my brother? Well. About that, I have just one thing to say."

When I paused, his brows rose in anticipation. "And that is…"

I threw my arms around his neck and illustrated my presentation with kisses. "Thank you! Thank you! Thank you!"

❧ Chapter 4 ❧

MY THIRD LIFE OFFICIALLY BEGINS

IN THE MIDST of the troubles in Arkentak, Mimma and I forged ahead with the wedding plans.

She had a clear vision for her firstborn's wedding, and my giving her free rein made her the happiest mother in the world. As promised, she checked with me before making any decisions, but I don't believe I objected to a single detail. I did, however, make a couple of small suggestions—the font size on the invitations, the color of the ribbons in some of the flower arrangements—so she'd see I really did care.

As happy as she was to have charge of it all, her delight couldn't compare to mine at not having to deal with it.

IN FREEMANSLAND, MARRIAGE is made through a legal contract. No ceremony required.

City wedding customs vary from place to place and from class to class. A wedding between Citizens by Merit tends to be more elaborate than what the common people do. Weddings among

Citizens by Commerce are even more extravagant. With Citizens First Class, however, weddings are often simple affairs. The CFCs see no need for pomp and theatrics, for they have nothing to prove.

Approaching Sentinel Pines in the family limo, I marveled at the difference between the estate now, in the summer, and when I'd first seen it in its shroud of snow.

A colorful pavilion rose on the grounds, with green vines climbing its upright beams. Lengths of white filmy fabric hung from both sides of the ridgepole, draping gracefully among the rafters to form a billowy roof.

A stage would be erected at one end, in front of the fountain. Seats would be arranged for the guests, and ropes of flowers would bedeck the whole thing. Workmen were even now setting up another tent where the food would be served.

It would be a small wedding by City standards, with only a hundred guests in all. A mere six of these would be guests of the bride: Jeriah and his family, and Uncle Rhe and Aunt Lanie. I'd invited the cousins, but they all begged off, claiming to have other engagements. More likely, though, they wanted nothing to do with a Cityslime marrying into the family.

I didn't blame them for that.

The car drove up the lane to the house, giving me a different view of it all. But no matter how I looked at it, none of it seemed real. I was getting married. Marrying into one of the proudest, most influential families in the world. Tomorrow, I would become a Citizen First Class through marriage.

I didn't care about citizenship. All I wanted was to spend the rest of my life with the man I loved and prove myself worthy of his name.

I SPENT THE morning of the wedding day in my suite, engulfed by a fluttering flock of attendants who cleaned and shaved and lotioned my body, styled my hair, crafted my face, perfected my already-perfect nails on hands and feet, and dressed me with the utmost care.

If I were like most brides, I'd have a friend with me for the preparations who would also accompany me to the ceremony. But the only person I'd want with me at a time like this was Seena, and she would be too uncomfortable in these surroundings. I didn't want to ask her.

Grey said a friend's participation was customary, but not required. "That's good, then," I'd told him. "I'll skip that part. And anyway, I don't need a friend. I'm used to being alone."

His response might not have been called a smile, but the corners of his eyes crinkled and his mustache turned up. "That will soon be a thing of the past."

As it happened, I was hardly alone that morning anyway. My myriad attendants gave me no peace.

When the pedicurist picked up my first foot, she yelped and dropped it back into the soaking tub. I'd forgotten to warn her about my many scars. Some were from cutting myself on sharp rocks and briars, but most were the telltale marks of parasitic mudworm maggots. Gran had taught me from the time I was a toddler how to dig them out with a katter thorn, so my infestations never became crippling. But the balls of my feet and the areas between my toes were riddled with tiny craters. Mudworm scars were common as nose hairs on Freemansland, but I guessed the people who attended to CFCs didn't usually run across that sort of thing.

The girl recovered her composure and resumed her work, and I didn't bother to explain. Let her wonder.

Eventually the beauty team's labors were complete, and I stood before the three-way mirror in the suite's monstrosity of a closet to survey the results.

My dark brown hair was swept loosely away from my face, except for a casual spiral allowed to escape on either side. A braid woven with flowers formed a crown, and the remainder of the tresses were captured at the back of my head in a choreographed shower of curls.

The brocaded-silk dress of pale sea foam green shimmered with tiny pearls. The bodice was high-necked with diagonal pleats in the back and horizontal draping in the front. My sleeves hugged the arm to the elbow, then blossomed into wrist-length, accordion-pleated bells trimmed with pearls. The floor-skimming skirt, smooth in front and gently bustled in back, made me feel I was swimming in luxury. Other than the Kentakian koorma, all my other clothes had legs, from my uniform culottes to everyday outfits to the wide-legged trousers of the tailor-made dresses Grey had bought me.

My shoes were flat—that was one thing I insisted on in my discussions with Mimma—open-toed, crisscrossed with ropes of pearls and flowers. The make-up artist was truly an artist, making my blue eyes the focus of attention and miraculously hiding my skin's many small scars and imperfections.

No one could guess I'd clawed my way out of the stillwater like a moss-grown reptile.

I was speechless. But a glance around at my attendants told me they expected me to say something, so I said the first thing that came to mind. "Ashgrey will be proud to call me his own."

The ladies beamed. Their livelihoods depended on pleasing people like the Standtalls.

"I'm very pleased," I added. I, soon to be a Standtall.

They curtseyed. "Thank you, ma'am."

A knock at the door drew our attention. "Would you get that, please?" I asked the manicurist, who stood nearest the doorway.

"Of course, ma'am."

She hurried to the front room, and I gathered my skirts and followed, with the other attendants forming a train behind me.

In the sitting room, the estate steward, Starham, stood just inside the door. Seeing me, his eyes widened for a half second before he recovered himself. "If you're ready, madam, I've been asked to escort you down."

I smiled. "I'm ready."

And I was. Though I'd never been to a wedding before, CFC or otherwise, Mimma and Grey had made sure I knew how to play the part of bride.

Treating me like a princess, Starham ushered me through the maze of a house to a rear exit, then into a curtained litter. That's what they called it, though it had wheels and a motor and wasn't carried by men like the old-fashioned kind. This was a conveyance made specifically for weddings, driven by two coachmen dressed in brilliant green.

The curtains on the right and left sides of the enclosure were on hinged rails, designed to swing out like double doors. When closed, they hid me from view—and prevented me from seeing where I was going. Bouncing across the lawn blindly on a cushioned bench in a tiny enclosure was a little weird, but I knew my destination and trusted the Standtalls' people to get me there safely.

After a slow, bumpy ride, the vehicle stopped. The enclosure in which I rode lowered to the ground, and a coachman climbed from his seat and stood outside the curtain. "Ready to disembark, madam?"

"I am."

The coachmen helped me exit the litter and guided me to the enclosure at the stage end of the pavilion. I heard the murmur of the guests' voices above the soft music, but I was hidden from their view.

There was nowhere to sit in this curtained room—I was impressed at the volume of fabric a wedding necessitated—so I stood. I knew that on the opposite side of the stage, Grey waited in an identical enclosure. Envisioning him pacing the small space, nearly bursting with anticipation, I smiled. I was nearly bursting too, but I didn't wear my emotions on my sleeve the way he did.

I hadn't been there for more than a minute—probably just long enough for my litter and Grey's to move out of sight—when the music changed. The voices hushed, the curtains drew back, and, recognizing our cue, Grey and I each walked onto the stage.

The guests rose, and a little voice shrilled, "Yook, yook! That's Auntie Jem!"

A ripple of amusement passed through the pavilion, but I didn't dare look out. For one thing, I was afraid seeing all those people out there would wake me up to reality and freeze me solid with terror. But more than that, the sight of Grey walking toward me arrested my full attention.

He would have caught the eye of any woman in range, in his deep green tailcoat with velvet collar. The velvet stripe on the matching trousers accented the length of his powerful frame. His vest was made from the same fabric as my dress, though it wasn't studded with pearls, and a filmy white ascot completed the look. It was a fine look indeed. And the man whose it was, was all mine.

From either side of the stage, we walked to a small table in front of the fountain. We each pulled out a chair and sat. That was the cue for the audience to take their seats as well.

Once everyone was settled, he spoke. "My betrothed."

I answered, "My love."

He pulled the chain holding the key from around his neck. I gave him my left hand, and he unlocked my bracelet. As he opened it and removed it from my wrist, he said, "I love you. And because I love you I release you. Fly if you wish."

I withdrew my hand, then slowly rose, keeping my eyes on his face.

All this followed a script, but I was aware it was all too real. I felt Jeriah's silent pleading in the front row. *Do it! This is your chance! Run!*

Should I?

As was the tradition, I took a step back, then turned as if to flee. My mind followed the thread of probable results if I did, in fact, take advantage of this gift of freedom. Initially, everyone's shocked dismay. (*What did you expect? She's a Freeman.*)

The professional consequences? Unthinkable. As Minister of Domestic Peace, Stalwart Standtall was over all the armed forces. It would not be wise to insult him.

But worst of all were the personal ramifications: I would be alone forever. And the tall, noble man who loved me would be crushed like a bird in the jaws of a dragon.

After three steps away—two more than tradition called for—I turned toward him again and resumed the script. "I cannot." And then adlibbed, "I will flee when fish fly."

The tension in the audience was palpable when I took those three strides away. They'd released a collective sigh of relief when I turned back. They tittered with laughter at my variation on the traditional wording. And they applauded as I returned to the script. "How can I leave the one who holds my heart in his hands?"

I hurried back to Grey, who had risen in dismay when I began to leave. At my return, he came around from the table—also a variation from the traditional interpretation of the dance—and drew me into his arms, causing the guests' applause to turn to cheers.

I didn't look out at their faces, but I couldn't help but wonder if Jeriah and Seena were frowning.

Let them. I'd made my decision, and confirmed it anew this day.

I sat back down, and instead of sitting opposite me as he was supposed to, Grey knelt on one knee before me. The audience *ah'd* with delight.

He pulled the platinum wedding band from his pocket and, with trembling hands, enclosed the chain bracelet within it. "Allow me, then, to give you this token of my undying love."

I extended my left hand and he first kissed it—again, a variant from tradition that delighted the audience—before clasping the band around my wrist. "Before these witnesses, I hereby declare that you are mine. As long as I live, I shall give you, Jemima, and only you, the honor, protection, provision, and affection that is due the wife of Ashgrey Standtall."

I took his clasped hands in both of mine and, looking into his glimmering glaffcrim eyes, concentrated on keeping my voice steady. "Before these witnesses, I hereby declare that you are mine. As long as I live, I, Jemima, shall give you, and only you, Ashgrey, the honor, defense, nurture, and affection that is due you as my husband."

A tear escaped a corner of his eye, and he didn't wipe it away. Clasping hands, we rose together and turned to face the guests.

"You are witnesses. Do you confirm this union?"

They stood and answered with happy certainty. "We do."

When they applauded, I allowed myself to search the audience, and my eye immediately met Jeriah's.

He applauded politely. But he wasn't smiling.

No matter. The platinum bracelet hung heavy on my arm. I was Mrs. Ashgrey Standtall, CFC, and there was nothing anyone could do to reverse that.

That window had closed forever.

❧ Chapter 5 ❧

FREEMANSLANDERS IN THE CITY

A T THE CEREMONY'S conclusion, Grey's smooth, warm hand holding my cold fingers gave me a sense of calm stability as we stepped down from the stage. Without that assurance, I may not have been able to face the guests crowding around to congratulate us.

Grey's parents began the process, embracing us both and welcoming me into the family. Beaming with delight, they stepped aside and allowed my nearest relations to do the same. In the absence of parents, that meant my brother and his wife.

I'm sorry to say my new husband and Jeriah didn't seem impressed with one another, but I can't fault Grey. He approached my brother with openness and the intent to befriend him, but Riah was barely polite as he shook his hand and muttered, "Congratulations." Even the hug he gave me seemed stiff and formal. Seena was courteous, but I got the impression she welcomed the need to occupy herself with the kids so she didn't have to really look at Grey.

My aunt and uncle, on the other hand, seemed entirely at ease rubbing shoulders with the wealthy and powerful. After greeting them, I pointed out Mimma's brother-in-law, Cago Talpin. "Uncle Rhe, I've heard you say you'd like to meet the Agricultural Minister face to face. Well, today's your chance, because he's right over there. Would you like me to introduce you?"

Uncle Rhe's blue eyes grew wide. "Is that the Minister? Seriously?"

"The very same. I met him the first time I visited Sentinel Pines, and he's surprisingly approachable. I can—"

"No need. I'll introduce myself." Before the last word was out of his mouth, Uncle Rhe was weaving his way through the other guests in a determined beeline toward Grey's uncle.

Aunt Lanie struggled after him in her high heels. "Rhe, wait. You can't just go barging your way—"

He paused and waited for her. "We're fine, Lanie. Jem said he's approachable, didn't she?"

I'd have gone too, but Grey's brother's children engulfed us in bouncing hugs, with their parents right behind.

Bark didn't bounce, but he gave Grey a massive embrace while Pearl peeled her children off us.

Bark gave me a less violent hug than he'd given Grey and kissed my cheek. "Welcome to the family. I mean that, truly. But hey, when you retire from the service, you should go into acting. You're a natural on the stage. We were all having heart palpitations at your performance."

Pearl embraced me too. "He's right, Jemma. It was *so* romantic!"

I managed to respond appropriately while keeping an eye on my uncle. Diminutive and sun-wizened, the intrepid glaffcrim farmer introduced himself to the towering official.

Earlier, Grey's Uncle Cago had told me he looked forward to meeting Uncle Rhe, as he was hopelessly addicted to Mol crim. So I wasn't surprised when a smile crossed his face upon learning who was accosting him. But I became concerned when Uncle Rhe's voice, too big for his small body, boomed across the crowd. "I'm happy to meet you at last, Minister. I've had a bone to pick with you for years."

The minister seemed amused as he sized up the little man before him. He said something, but I couldn't catch the words.

I debated if it might be advisable to excuse myself and go intervene, but Uncle Cago shook Rhe's hand in a friendly manner. Next minute they were introducing their wives, and the four were soon conversing as if they were next-door neighbors.

It may have been the first time Freemanslanders had ever attended a CFC function as guests rather than servants, but my family pulled it off with aplomb.

I floated through the afternoon with a poise and confidence that surprised me. In the back of my mind I wondered if I were acting a part, as I'd first thought, or if I was truly becoming the person I pretended to be. Either way, it felt good.

Together Grey and I spoke with each guest, ate plenty, and drank a little. Yes, just a little. I was careful to limit myself.

I couldn't help but notice Riah went through quite a few glasses, though. At least he shared my ability to handle alcohol gracefully. It loosened him up a bit, but not enough to cause any raised eyebrows.

Except for Seena's, when he started flirting with two of Grey's teenaged cousins. That was when she grabbed him and dragged him away, handing Jeo to him while they said their goodbyes.

"It was a lovely wedding," she told me, avoiding Grey's eye. "Thank you for inviting us. We'd like to stay longer, but the kids need a nap."

Some of the other guests had small children too, and the Standtalls had made arrangements for them in the house. But I didn't press Riah and Seena to stay. "We're so glad you were able to come," I said instead.

Grey said he was sorry to see them go, and I sent them off with hugs all around, even though Jeo fussed and pushed me away. I wondered vaguely if I should feel guilty for being glad they were gone.

⁂

I'M TOLD THE party continued well into the night, but toward evening, Grey and I slipped out.

One of the CFC wedding traditions involved the bride and groom trying to sneak away while the guests do their best to prevent them. It was a game, and sometimes the plots and subplots grew quite involved.

When Mimma told me about it, I said, "That sounds like fun." Because it did. And because I was good at Stealth and would probably be able to slip away despite the most devious of strategies to prevent it. But I didn't care to play the game with Grey. Though he had too many good qualities to count, where Stealth was concerned, he was an oaf.

"But I'm not sure I want to conclude my wedding that way," I added. "Is it required?"

"Oh, no, of course not." She chuckled. "I think Ashgrey would prefer to dispense with it as well. He seems to think it undignified."

So Mimma let the guests know we preferred to avoid any intrigue.

We found our chance to make a break when Bark entertained everyone with a funny situation involving a co-star on the set of his video show. While he held their attention, Grey and I edged away, then scampered hand in hand across the lawn to where a car waited, our luggage already loaded. The driver and footman opened the doors, and we slid in.

Grey took me into his arms. "This is the best day of my life."

I let him kiss me despite the two men getting into the front seat. "I can't recall a better one myself."

The limo drove down the lane. The sun had lowered behind the trees, and the lights went on in the pavilion. The fixtures were part of the decorations, and Mimma was eager to see them lit, but she'd instructed the groundskeepers to wait until we'd made our escape. Now the pavilion blazed like a sun.

Grey spoke to the driver. "Stop a moment, would you please? And open the sunroof?"

The driver complied, and Grey instructed him to blow the horn as he pulled me up to stand, head and shoulders extending through the sunroof. The car horn drew the guests' attention, everyone shouted and waved, "Goodbye!" and Grey and I waved back with both arms. He called, "Thank you, everyone!" then ducked back inside, pulling me down with him.

He told the driver, "Okay, we can go now," and off we went to the airport.

We boarded one of the Standtall planes and made the two-hour flight to the family's retreat, Quarry House, in Noblin Woods. Though a fraction of the size of the mansion at Sentinel Pines, it could have comfortably housed several families. That week, however, we had it all to ourselves except for the staff—and they were instructed to keep out of sight unless they were needed.

Like the rest of the house, the master suite was elaborately rustic. The driver and footman carried up our luggage, said, "Good evening, Mr. and Mrs. Standtall," and exited.

Grey removed his jacket and draped it over the back of a chair. "That was an excellent dinner we had on the plane, but would you like some dessert? We have ice cream."

"That's not fair. You know I'd do anything for ice cream."

He loosened his cravat. "I know." He smiled, arching his eyebrows suggestively. "That's rather the point." Without waiting for my reply—which I was trying to come up with but utterly failing—he turned and disappeared into the next room.

I didn't follow right away. As much as I loved Grey, this whole wedding night thing had me nervous. But at the sound of a freezer opening, I couldn't keep my feet from going after him. In the kitchen area, he bent over to take something from the bottom of the freezer.

I decided I liked that view of my husband.

He straightened, holding one stemmed glass in each hand, and closed the freezer door with his knee. The stripe on the trouser really did accent the length of those limbs. "Let's take it out onto the balcony. I seem to remember you like this flavor. Cabernet with raspberry?"

"Mmm, you remember right."

He set the dishes on the counter, then opened a nearby door. "They're supposed to have sprayed for insects, so it shouldn't be too buggy."

I started to pick up one of the ice creams, but he shooed me away. "Go on out and get comfortable. I'll bring it."

I stepped onto the balcony and sat at the small round table. Grey brought out the glasses, along with spoons and napkins. Then he brought the other chair so close that when he sat, our legs touched.

It was a warm night. A quarter moon looked down on us and seemed to smile. The dark-shrouded woods below rang with insect song, and flickerflies chased one another around the edge of the trees. But only the occasional moth fluttered near the balcony.

Grey reached his spoon in front of me and took ice cream from my bowl.

"Hey, that's mine."

"There is no *mine* anymore." He slid the spoonful into his mouth. "As of today, everything is ours."

He wasn't talking about ice cream, of course. That word *everything* encompassed Sentinel Pines, Quarry House and the woods beyond, the family holdings all over the world—and the power that came with the Standtall name.

The thought gave me no delight. I picked up my spoon. "I didn't marry you for what you have, you know."

"I know that." The corners of his eyes smiled.

"I don't care about your money. Or about being a CFC."

He nodded. "I know that."

I was glad he didn't ask me what I *did* care about, because I was afraid to admit it, even to myself. "I'm not sure if I can handle... everything—" I waved the spoon in a gesture to indicate the entirety of things. "I'd rather it stayed just yours. It's too much to deal with." I stuck my spoon into the bowl in front of him. "All I want is ice cream." I ate a mouthful.

What *did* I want? To be loved. That's why I married him. I loved him, because he loved me.

He had no idea what was going through my mind. "You're a fast learner. Unless I miss my guess, you'll know to handle *everything* in no time." He waved his spoon as I had. "I'll help you. But first, let me help you with this." He took another dab from my bowl and fed me a spoonful. "What do you think? Do you like this one better?" He gestured from my bowl to his. "Or that?"

"They're exactly the same. But I like this one better." I tapped the bowl in front of me. "You know why?"

"Why?"

I fed him a taste from the bowl in front of him. "Because it tastes better from your spoon."

Licking his lips, he shook his head. "No, it's better from your spoon."

I put on a thoughtful expression. "I'm not so sure. Let's try that again."

We fed one another alternately from one bowl and then the other, leaning closer and closer, until we were almost in the same chair.

When both bowls were empty, he said, "Is your mouth cold?"

"Of course it is." What kind of a question was that?

"Let me warm it with mine."

Oh. *That* kind of question. I rather liked the suggestion, and we warmed one another's mouths for the next couple of minutes. Then I laid my head on his chest and listened to his heartbeat.

"Are you ready, Mrs. Standtall?"

I sat up. I knew what he meant, but the question made me tense. Uncertain. I played with a strand of his hair where it curled behind his ear.

"Our luggage is out there in the sitting room. Are you ready for me to... carry it in?"

His smile was gentle. Wistful. Undemanding.

Still fingering his hair, I studied his face a moment, thinking about it. Then I kissed him again. "Yes, Mr. Standtall. I'm ready."

❧ Chapter 6 ❧

QUARRY HOUSE

I BOBBED IN the quarry lake, squinting against the afternoon sunlight that sparked off the ripples.

After a moment of admiring my husband's muscular form as he swam, I dove under him and came up on the other side, startling him.

He laughed. "No wonder you love to eat fish. You are one."

"That would make me a cannibal, wouldn't it?"

He treaded water. "Ever eat a fish named Freeman?"

"There are no fish named Freeman."

"Well, then, you're not a cannibal. But you're also wrong, because you, my dear, are a fish named Freeman. That was formerly your name, anyway."

I dove again and couldn't hear what he was saying.

Under the water, I tickled his feet, and he kicked me away. When I came up, I asked, "What did you say?"

"I said quit nibbling on my toes, you Freeman fish."

"That's not what you said."

He wiped water from his eyes and shook his head. "I said I like the name Freeman. I just might keep calling you that."

"You *like* it?"

"I do. Because it describes you. You're free of pretention. Of convention. You're free to be your own woman and you don't care what anyone thinks."

I considered. "I care what you think."

"Glad to hear it. But right now, I think I'd like to race you to the island." He took off for the shore.

"What? You like to lose?"

He had a superior wingspan, but I had the advantage of being a fish. I won, of course. Nobody beat me at swimming.

First thing that morning, Grey had introduced me to a sport he called trailing. Or maybe it's only a sport if you compete with someone else. Which he didn't, because I was no competition. Trailing consisted of riding a PTV, or Personal Trail Vehicle, along winding, steep, rutted, trails through the overgrown woods as fast as you could, as noisily as you could, until you killed yourself. He called this fun.

There were several PTVs at Quarry House, and he showed me how to drive one. We went up and down the road a couple times until I was comfortable with it. Then he yelled, "Follow me!" and led the way into the woods.

That's when I realized why we were wearing all that gear: heavy pants with knee pads, sturdy long-sleeved shirt, boots, gloves, helmet, and goggles. Even I, who loved hot weather, thought it all those clothes were too warm. But once I started bouncing along after him, I was glad of their protection. In fact, I'd have preferred more extensive armor.

Better yet, to not be doing this at all.

I had no intention of keeping up with his rate of speed, and before long, he was out of sight. Not out of earshot, though. The woods cringed at the noise we both made.

Moving at a more sane velocity, I rounded a bend and found him waiting. He shouted over the rumble of our engines. "Am I going too fast for you?"

"Not if it's your plan that we both die today. But I, for one, would like to enjoy our marriage for more than twenty-four hours."

He laughed. "I didn't think you were afraid of anything."

"What's fear got to do with it? I'm just being sensible."

He shook his head. "Okay, we can take it slow if you want. And I'll stick to the easier trails."

I'd have rather done something else instead. But maybe if I rode a little more, I'd learn to like it. "Sounds good." I tested my helmet to make sure it was on securely. "Let's go."

We rode all morning, then went back to the house. "How'd you like it?" Grey asked as we put the equipment away.

"I like swimming better."

So that's what we did after lunch.

We spent a week at Quarry House. The best week of my life—of the first three lives, anyway.

The second day, Grey suggested motorcycling, but I couldn't stomach the thought. I told him to go ahead and ride—I'd spend my time exploring the area on foot. So while he risked his neck dashing around on two wheels like a maniac, I risked mine climbing cliffs, almost causing him to wreck when he happened to see me from the trail.

That was the first and last time that week we went our separate ways.

We swam. We picnicked. We hiked together—no cliff climbing that day. When the weather was stormy, he taught me a complicated strategy game called Invade and Conquer played with various cards and tokens and money vouchers. It took a good bit of time and effort before I learned the rules. I liked the mental challenge of the game, but not the history upon which the game play was based. That is, the City Fathers' ruthless takeover of the planet in slow but inexorable increments.

Whatever we did, indoors or out, we talked. About everything. About nothing.

Having met his family and visited their estates, I could picture the stories he told me. Growing up a Standtall was altogether foreign to my experience, but I could visualize it.

He didn't do as well with the stories I told. How could a man hate his own daughter? Grey couldn't fathom toddler twins being left on their own while the adults worked elsewhere. And a little girl living alone in the woods, less afraid of dragons and swamp bears than the dangers that lurked at home? Stealing her father's homemade whisky so she could drink away the pain? Not wearing clothes, no regular meals, no education?

Grey didn't doubt the truth of my tales, but his privileged mind couldn't process it.

I never did tell him about Mayne. Not that week, and not ever. Mentally, I buried Mayne in an unmarked grave. I no longer hated him, but the thought of him brought a stab of guilt. I thought if Grey never knew of him, I wouldn't have to explain. Explain how Mayne had always loved me, but I'd never realized it. Protected me. Wooed me, even when I was too scared and stupid to respond. He'd enabled me to escape Freemansland, and I hated him for it. And now... he might actually be waiting for me, as Riah had said. Brave, loyal, faithful, ever-steady Mayne.

No. I wouldn't think about it. And it was the one thing I never told Grey.

The first two evenings, we watched television together, something I wasn't in the habit of doing. We started off watching every episode yet released of his brother's new drama. Though the show itself didn't interest me, it was fun to see Bark perform on the screen. We watched other shows the second night, and it all seemed like mere noise to me. I told him I'd rather read a book.

That was fine, because there were plenty of them around the house. Grey put in an earpiece so the television didn't distract me, and I lay on the couch with my head in his lap to read.

Even when it rained, we didn't play Invade and Conquer *all* day. Sometimes we left the game on the kitchen table and moved our play into the bedroom. We were newlyweds, after all.

Our last morning at Quarry House, I awoke to the sound of a roencaw honking outside the window, hailing his lover in the misty dawn. She squawked a reply from a distance away, and he called her in. The back-and-forth cries went on for a couple of minutes, her voice growing closer all the while, until their squawks changed to coos.

I snuggled against my lovebird. He must have been listening too, for he said, "Would you like me to sing to you like that?"

I smiled. "I'd love it if you'd sing to me. You have a nice voice. But I don't need you to honk like a roencaw."

And so, of course, he did. And I answered with a poor imitation of the female's caw. We went back and forth a couple of times, laughing, until I asked, "You know what I was thinking?"

"That we should take this show on the road?"

"No." My giggle died away, but a smile lingered. "That I'm beginning to understand—just beginning, mind you—how sex and worship are related."

I could almost hear his intellect spark with interest. "Explain."

"Sex—that is, when properly done. I mean, in love. Not slotting. Slotting is someth—"

He went tense. "Whoa, stop right there."

"I'm sorry, you don't like my choice of words?"

"I do not. I realize it's a habit for you, and I knew your penchant for profanity when I asked you to marry me. But now that we are married, I'd like you leave the gutter talk in the gutter, okay? Because that's all behind you now."

"Gladly." I knew old habits weren't easy to break, but at that moment, in that place, anything seemed possible. And I truly did want to please him.

"So you were saying?"

"Yes. I was saying..." I paused to pull my thoughts back together. "Lovemaking, as opposed to that which I shall not now name, is an expression of our devotion."

"Um hm..."

"We give our bodies to one another as a sacrificial offering. You know, like a religious devotee offers sacrifice to his god. We worship one another."

His whiskers, left untrimmed since arriving at Quarry House, caught in my hair as he smiled. "That's quite a thought."

"Is it true, professor?"

"When it's properly done, as you say, I think you're right."

I knew what he was thinking, so I said it for him. "But when the person giving the sacrifice is unwilling? When the one performing the act does it out of anger, or of love for himself, not the other?"

He let his breath out slowly, rubbing my back. "Yes. What is it then?"

"It's worship too, but blasphemous. It's a good thing gone wrong in the worst kind of way. It hurts everyone."

He didn't say anything, but his caresses continued with greater tenderness.

"But you know what else?"

He grunted. "Hmm?"

"*True* worship brings healing. It transforms." I spoke slowly as the words rose out of nowhere and took form in my mind. "Love confronts the false and reveals the blasphemy for what it is. It shows what could be. What should be." Though unsure of what I was saying, I felt certain it was true. "It points to what *will* be."

He shifted position to look at me, and when I turned my face toward him, he covered it with kisses. "That's amazing. Where do you get this stuff?"

"From you."

His kisses then reached my mouth and stopped the rest of my words. But when his lips moved on, I finished the thought. "I learn a great deal from you, professor."

☀

And then it was time to go home.

"Home" being military housing in Yarapit provided by the Land Forces for married couples.

You remember Yarapit, right? With the smell and the dampness and the rat in the flour bin? The home provided for Grey and me, being officers, was better than that, but not much. We didn't have a canal that doubled as a sewer flowing past our door, but our house was damp, drab, and peeling, the floors sloped, the walls were warped, and the smell of rot lay over all.

Oh, yeah. There were rats, too. And enough insects to make a squeamish person lose her mind.

But I wasn't squeamish. Even after spending the past week in the luxury of Quarry House, I only chafed a little at having to shift mental gears and live again in such conditions.

Grey wasn't squeamish, either. But as a pigeonhead, he didn't think he should have to put up with the squalor. Before our marriage, when he saw where we'd be living, he'd put in a request to be moved to habitable quarters. The answer came back promptly:

Request denied. The housing he'd been assigned was the best available in Yarapit. End of story.

So, shortly before the wedding, we'd moved our things in. Grey's reaction alarmed me a little. I'd seen him upset before, but nothing like the tirade he unleashed as we surveyed the shabby rooms. At one point, I thought he'd put a fist through something.

His exclamations ran the gamut: *The smell around here makes me gag.* (This in reference to the whole vicinity, not just the home's interior.) *Are those rat droppings? Something's built a nest in the closet. The way the walls lean, I'll be surprised if they don't fall in and crush us.* He summed it up with final, "I'm not bringing my new bride home to a place like this."

I saw what he saw and smelled what he smelled, but it didn't bother me anywhere near as much as his behavior did. "Your bride has seen a lot worse."

He stared at me a moment before answering. "That was then. You shouldn't have to put up with this after we're married. This is terrible. I need to at least hire someone to give this place a thorough cleaning."

"What? We can't bring an outside cleaning service in here."

The compound was under tight security. The only people going in and out were military personnel—or, if necessary, utility workers or other civilians whose services were required, and then only under close guard. Professional housecleaners weren't given access.

His heavy brow grew even heavier, and he looked ready to unleash a string of epithets that would make a Freemanslander proud. But all he said, through clenched teeth, was, "What. The. Glish."

"What do we need them for? We can clean it."

You'd have thought I'd said we could grow gills and live underwater. "How are we going to do that?"

"Same way the professionals would, except we won't get paid for it."

Cleaning was never anything I did for fun, but I knew how to do it, thanks first to Aunt Lanie and then to my four years at the Academy. So together, we bought the necessary supplies and went to work.

If you've never seen a CFC cleaning a shower or washing walls, you've missed a rare sight. But after hours of toil, the place looked a lot better. We set out rat poison and fumigated for insects, then brought in all the furniture from his apartment. My little flat came furnished, so I only had to bring my clothing and personal things.

Though the results of our efforts were reasonably satisfying, Grey wasn't placated. He was certain by the time we came home from Quarry House, rodents would have chewed up the furniture, our clothes would be full of moths, and roaches would be building condominiums in the kitchen cabinets.

That's why, when we headed for home at the end of the week, his buoyant mood didn't make the trip with him. Boarding the plane for Yarapit, he was so dark with gloom he was short with one of the flight attendants.

After trying to make it up to her with uncharacteristic friendliness, I settled in the seat beside him and squeezed his arm. "I know, our house isn't very nice. But it's temporary. We'll be okay until you can get a transfer."

"Okay? Didn't you say even Seena couldn't take it in Yarapit?"

I narrowed my eyes. "What do you mean, *even Seena?*"

He scowled. "I just meant if your brother's wife refused to live there, why shouldn't I be allowed to object?"

I knew what he meant, and it wasn't that. He'd meant, *Even Seena, the dowdy little Freemanslander who wouldn't know a palace from a pigsty.* But he was upset enough already—unreasonably so, in my opinion—that I saw no point in irritating him further by telling him how wrong he was. "As long as we're together, I don't care where we live."

His glaffcrim eyes searched my face, and his voice softened. "You really mean that, don't you?"

"Of course I do. I already told you, I don't care about money or houses or things. I just want to be with you."

He sighed. "I need to be more like you."

I almost laughed. What a thought!

❧ Chapter 7 ❧

BOOM

AFTER GREY AND I were betrothed, the Division moved him out of the Eyes-On unit—those of us who gathered information by physically spying on people—and put him in Cyber Squad.

It was such a good fit, I'm not sure why he was in Eyes-On to begin with. In both units, though, he had a gift for organization and analysis, seeing the big picture and reading between the lines. He knew how to focus the sharp minds working beneath him to hone in on what was important and not be distracted by side issues.

Even before he went into Cyber, he felt sure the rebels had sympathizers everywhere, and it drove him nuts that others couldn't see it as well. That concern precipitated my presentation to the Council at Saltpoint Creek, which I already told you about.

What I didn't mention was the result of that meeting.

The Council was, as Grey had hoped, shaken from their complacency. But while some were prodded to action, others were provoked to resentment. A certain amount of rancor arose against the Minister and his busybody son who had the poor taste to marry a Freeman. They also resented the upstart he married.

Who knew being a Citizen First Class was no guarantee against danger?

⁂

HOME TO YARAPIT.

When we exited the autocab outside the house, Grey sniffed the air. "Still smells like a sewer."

Our marriage had hardly begun, and I was already tired of his grouchiness. "Did you think that would magically change?"

He set his jaw as if biting off a retort as we carried our bags to the front stoop. He unlocked the door, then opened it, slowly, and motioned for me to stay behind him.

I stood on the stoop and waited, not because I was afraid of what was inside, but hoping he'd see how ridiculous his fears were.

He stepped through the doorway, and I heard a, "Hmmph."

I stayed where I was.

"What are you doing out there? Get in here."

I dutifully crossed the threshold. "I was waiting for you to clear the area. The way you were acting, I'm surprised you didn't draw your gun before going in."

"Ha ha, funny. But look, the place is the same as when we left it."

"What a surprise."

He turned to me, brows raised. "Since when did you become a smart mouth?"

I shrugged. "Since you became a whiner. You've been doing nothing but grumble since we left Quarry House."

He frowned and opened his mouth to speak, but apparently changed his mind. Then he waved toward the still-open door. "Let's go." He ushered me back out onto the stoop.

I let him guide me out. "What are you doing?"

"We're going to do this again, but the right way this time." He turned me around to face him. "Okay." He straightened his shoulders. "Now. Here we are, my dear. Home at last." He plastered on a too-cheery smile.

Playing along, I bounced on my toes and clapped. "May we go in? I can't wait!"

"Yes, indeed." He took me by the hand, and we entered. "A lovely place, isn't it?" He gestured. "A cozy little sitting room with a sofa, two chairs, and, oh, look at this. A 200-centimeter video screen and an almost-new media streaming system, so you can keep up with all your favorite shows."

"For me? How thoughtfuls!" Then I laughed and threw my arms around his neck. "But I can think of things I'd rather do, can't you?"

"If you'd like." He kissed me. "But I think we should bring in our bags first."

☀

BEFORE LONG, it felt like we'd been married forever. Grey said the same thing—and he said it with satisfaction.

He couldn't reconcile himself to living in that house, though. He put in for a promotion, planning to request a transfer once he got his captain bars.

"Where do you want to go?" I asked.

"I don't care. Anywhere but here. Now that I'm in Cyber, I can work from anywhere. I don't see why I need to be in Yarapit."

I'd wondered that too, but it wasn't my main concern. "When they transfer you, what will happen to me?"

"You'll go with me, of course. We need Eyes-Ons everywhere."

I'd recently heard of two couples who had been split up and sent to different posts. The IA never used to do that, but the situation in Arkentak required a number of changes, none of them for the better. But I just smiled. "Let's hope you get that promotion soon."

Our work kept us busy. Serving in different units meant we didn't keep the same hours. Sometimes we barely saw each other for two or three days at a time, unless we could arrange to take meals together. When I had to leave Yarapit and put my eyes elsewhere, which happened more often than either of us would have liked, we'd be out of touch the whole time, as we couldn't risk our communications being intercepted.

Our primary purpose at that state of the conflict—indeed, the first priority of all the Division, everywhere—was ascertaining what entities and individuals outside Arkentak supported the rebels. The Enforcers made few arrests because the City wanted to follow the threads back to see how deeply they were woven into the fabric of the rest of the world. The information the Division acquired enabled the City to thwart an untold number of treasonous actions, but the primary objective was to determine who was pulling the strings of the various puppets we'd discovered. And often, that required us to leave those puppets on the stage.

ON ONE OCCASION, when on assignment in Dabamal, I took advantage of the opportunity to visit a spa. Not my old favorite, where I'd be recognized, but one on the other side of town.

In Yarapit, spas and men's clubs were off-limits to military personnel. Dabamal, however, was a little more secure, and there was no rule against it there.

I left the spa feeling refreshed and glad I'd taken the time to do it. It wasn't until I arrived back home late that night that I learned three armed rebels had entered that very spa just minutes after I'd left. Shouting their usual battle cry, "Centre City, begone! Kentak lives!" the men gunned down the customers. They didn't seem interested in the employees, though some of those were injured in the attack as well. Seven women died.

I didn't tell Grey I'd just been in there, because I had no desire to see him explode. But after that, I was more careful when I traveled.

Another thing I was careful about was keeping our humble house clean. It helped Grey deal with the miserable accommodations.

A few months into our marriage, we both had a day off at the same time. With no pressing reason to get up, we luxuriated in bed for a while, then got up and made a pot of glaffcrim. No matter what our living conditions, neither of us was willing to start the day without a good strong cup or two of genuine Moll.

After sitting at the table reviewing the newsfeed, Grey got up to refill his cup. "Ready for another?"

"I'd love one, thanks." I handed him my cup without looking up from my book.

A minute later, he returned and set the mug, full and billowing with fragrant steam, on the table in front of me. "I'm amazed this rat hole is still clean after all this time. It doesn't even stink bad enough to cover the scent of crim."

I thanked him for the cup, then looked up at him as he rounded the table to take his own seat. "You're kidding, right?"

"No. This place is as clean as it was the day we moved in. I can see I've been throwing good money away paying for weekly service the past fifteen years. A couple times a year would have been enough."

When I laughed, his expression turned puzzled, "What?"

"*I've* been cleaning it, you big silly. If I didn't do it every couple of days, we'd be wading in filth by now."

His eyes widened. "Really? When? I've never seen you."

Between the memory of him cleaning the shower, his dumbfounded look now, and the ridiculousness of his assumption that the house never got dirty, a wave of hilarity overtook me.

He wasn't amused, though. "What in the world is so funny?"

The way his heavy brow lowered over those dark eyes sobered me up fairly quickly. "Nothing." I took a deep breath to bring my laughter under control. "You should see yourself, is all. You looked so adorably confused."

"I am confused. I can't believe you've been cleaning this house all these months and I never knew it. You should—" He swallowed, and when he spoke again, his voice was strained, as if the words were hard to get out. "You should let me help you next time."

I stifled another laugh. "I hate the thought of spending what little time we have together cleaning house."

His furrowed brow eased with relief.

"As long as I keep up with it, it's not a big job. It gives me something to do when I'm home alone, and I'm happy to do it. You know why?"

He shook his head. "I can't imagine why *anyone* would be happy to do housecleaning."

"I know you'll never like this place, but when it's clean, you don't hate it so much. So I like doing it because it makes you happy."

He stared at me with an expression reminiscent of his father's sober, dark-eyed gaze. "It does make me happy. *You* make me happy. You amaze me, Freeman."

⁂

TWO WEEKS BEFORE our first wedding anniversary, Grey and I met for dinner at the officer's lounge before going our separate ways. He, to oversee the ongoing task of virtual snooping, and I, to the Division compound in Suthfan, near the Arkentak-Watland border. The Eyes-On commander there was concerned about sloppiness on the part of some of his people, and he called me in to do some training.

Grey had been putting in long hours and wasn't in the best of moods. I had no stomach for his grumpiness because I had concerns of my own. As a result, we did more eating than talking.

He chewed his last mouthful, gave his mustache a careful left-right wipe, and laid down his napkin. "I don't like this."

I glanced at his empty plate. "You ate it all."

He shook his head. "That wasn't very good either, but it's not what I meant. I don't like that it seems every time you travel, there's an attack somewhere near your location."

He was right. And though we hadn't discussed it before, it bothered me as well. Beginning with the shooting at the spa in Dabamal, my steps outside the compound were dogged by gunmen, fires, hazardous spills, and vehicle mishaps. In two cases, I had been near enough the action that I'd received minor injuries. The perpetrators usually died before being apprehended, but the two that the City was able to question both claimed not to know their true mission. They were merely operating under orders to commit this act at that place at such-and-such a time. If a specific person was targeted, they didn't seem to know it.

Grey said what I was thinking. "It's too coincidental."

"I know what you mean." I took a sip of pseudo-glaffcrim—the best we could get in Arkantak those days—and made a face at it. "I can't help but think..." I sighed. "I don't know. I'm probably imagining things."

His expression was serious. "I doubt that you are. What are you thinking?"

"I hesitate to say it." Though no one was listening, I leaned toward him across the table and lowered my voice. "I didn't make any friends when I gave that presentation at Saltcreek. I almost got the impression someone in the room—maybe even more than one—had connections here in Arkentak, and they didn't appreciate it that I spoke that possibility aloud. And..." I lowered my voice even more.

"General Denn was pretty open in blaming me for bringing down Colonel Redruff. If she's colluding with someone here in Arkentak herself, she wouldn't appreciate my suggestion that Redruff wasn't the only one."

He grunted. "That's occurred to me as well. But from what I can see, she's in the clear. She just doesn't like you because you're a Freeman. She thinks you should keep your nose out of CFC affairs."

"You've checked her out? Seriously?"

"To a degree. And whatever she may feel about you, her hatred of Daig Lar far exceeds it."

I drained my cup. "The High Priestess's husband? What's he got to do with anything?"

Grey hesitated. "Maybe nothing."

"But maybe something?"

He spoke so low I could hardly hear him. "Maybe everything." He cleared his throat. "Whoever's behind the trouble around here does seem to be—well, not targeting you, perhaps, but I don't like the coincidences."

"Neither do I. But what am I supposed to do? I can't very well tell Commander Thessar I don't want to go because I'm afraid somebody's trying to kill me."

Grey's dark eyes roved my face. "No, you can't. And I haven't been able to do anything either."

"You tried? You can't do that, it's—"

"No, no, I didn't break any regulations. I didn't even bend any." He reached across the table and took my hand in both of his. "I've been looking into the chatter surrounding those incidents and reading the reports on the investigations, and I'm not finding anything to connect them. Not to each other, and not to you."

"Maybe it's all just random, then. There are flare-ups everywhere these days, and I'm frequently sent to the hot spots."

"Maybe." He fingered my bracelet but looked into my eyes. "I know you have to go. I understand that. But be careful, Jemma. I don't know what I'd do if anything happened to you."

He usually called me Freeman, and the use of my first name in such a tender tone almost brought tears to my eyes. Or maybe I was just overtired. I smiled. "I don't know what I'd do either. But don't worry. I'll be fine."

It was a long train trip to Suthfan, and I didn't get much sleep. Something I'd eaten before I left disagreed with me, or maybe I was getting a stomach bug. I was sick enough to be miserable but not enough to be incapacitated. So I reported to the commander at the base as ordered despite feeling wan and exhausted.

I'm afraid I was a little short that day with the four Specialists I was supposed to be training, but who could blame me? I'd been under a lot of stress, living and working in what amounted to wartime conditions, though the City refused to call it that. I was so sick I could barely function, and the people I was supposed to be working with seemed to have rocks for brains. Major Gates and her team must be scraping the bottom of the barrel if these new Specialists were representative of the recruits they were bringing in these days.

The second day I felt a bit better. And because I was trying to be more honorable, like a proper Standtall, I even apologized to the Specialists for my impatience the day before. "We got off on the wrong foot yesterday," I said first thing, "and it's my fault. I've been fighting a stomach bug, and I'm afraid it got the better of me. So let's start over. I'll do my best to be more patient, and I'm asking you to give your best as well."

I recognized their expressions. It was the look I used to give to CFCs who were my superiors. Controlled disdain. Inner rebellion. Imagining what I'd like to do to the Cityslime if I had the opportunity, and if I could get away with it.

After the initial shock, I had to admit there was no reason why they shouldn't view me that way. My name was Standtall, wasn't it?

I stared at them right back.

"Of course, ma'am," they said, or something approximating it.

A wave of pain through my gut made me hold my breath for a moment. When the cramp ebbed, I said, "Good. Very well. This is what we're going to do." I tried to ignore another pain as I picked up my tablet. "I've devised an exercise that will give you an opportunity to put into practice some of the things we went over yesterday. You'll work together, but you'll be evaluated separately so we can see what aspects still need improvement."

So much for feeling better today. Steeling my jaw against the churning of my stomach, I squinted at the tablet until I located the document I'd been looking for, then sent it to the Specialists. "I've sent you the instructions." Another pain, sharper this time. "And I'm sorry, but I'm going to have to visit the restroom. Please review what I just sent you, and we'll get started when I get back."

I hurried out, thankful the bathroom wasn't far.

If it was a simple matter of eating something that disagreed with me, I should be over it by now. Was I sick? Or... I hated to think it, but had I been poisoned? I reviewed everything I'd eaten for the past forty-eight hours and tried to think who might have had access to it.

The symptoms had started on the train, but I didn't eat anything there. How about a drink? Yes, I'd had a couple of beers before trying to sleep, but they were sealed. It was unlikely anyone had tampered with them.

I went over everything, but couldn't think how this could be poisoning. It must merely be an illness. Did I know anyone else who was sick?

After a while, I thought it was probably safe to get up and leave, so I stood. But in the same moment I heard a rumble, an alarm went off, and someone shouted outside in the hall. I couldn't understand the words.

An ear-rending roar filled the air and sucked the wind from my lungs.

❧ Chapter 8 ❧

A LIVE ONE

LATER THAT DAY, a coalition of the inhabitants of the southern two-thirds of Arkentak—all the territory above Zapad and south of the Eel River, from Indopso on the west and Watland on the east—declared themselves to be the sovereign nation of Kentak, no longer under the authority of Centre City.

It was an act of treason such as the City had never seen.

I didn't know any of this, though, because I was buried beneath a pile of rubble. Barely alive, and only that thanks to the protection of one side of the metal bathroom stall.

Centre City issued a massive evacuation order that same evening. All citizens, military personnel, and employees had seventy-two hours to get out of Kentak. No exceptions. They recommended the residents of Zapad, Indopso, and Watland living near the borders move out of the way as well.

It was a massive undertaking, made all the more difficult by the great many who first had to be dug out of the rubble. Simultaneous missile attacks had been launched that morning against City installations and military compounds in twelve Kentan cities.

I imagine the people of the new Kentan nation cheered to see the City on the run. They must have gloated that the cry "Centre City, begone! Kentak lives!" had become a reality. The first stroke of the war must have seemed a great victory.

But at the time, I didn't know any of this.

Nor did I know how distraught Grey was. He tried to call me when he learned a missile had hit the base at Suthfan, but I didn't answer. His attempts to contact me continued to fail, and he was unable to learn anything from anyone else. All of Arkentak was in chaos.

Grey wanted to rush to Suthfan, but the safety of his people and the security of City technologies must be protected. He had no choice but to remain and oversee the evacuation of his unit. The base commander at Yarapit put it succinctly: "If she's alive, they'll find her. They're doing their jobs, Standtall, and we must do ours."

All I knew was that I was on the floor beneath a metal panel, with one end on the floor and the other supported by the toilet near my head. Above me, it bowed inward in an irregular lumpy pattern, which I guessed was made by pieces of building material falling on it. There wasn't much room under there.

My left arm and shoulder were killing me. So was my hip. Probably injured when I'd slammed against the hard floor. From the pounding in my head, it must have hit something too. Maybe the floor, maybe the toilet. For a long time I heard pieces of things falling, sometimes landing on the panel above me. Dust filtered down, but no light found its way in.

And my gut churned. I won't tell you the result of that.

Sirens. I remember muffled sirens at first. Then a relative silence, except for thuds and crashes as unseen things continued to fall. I lay there for a long time.

⁂

I LAY THERE for a long, long time.

Though my body was immobile, my mind went everywhere. I reviewed my life, tried to make sense out of it. Knew it would soon end.

Wanted Grey. Desperately wanted Grey. To hear his voice outside my prison, to see the battered panel lift, and light flow in framing his anxious face in the opening. I would smile. I would say, "It's about time you got here."

I would say, "I don't care where I am, as long as we're together."

We couldn't fit in that tiny space together, of course. He'd have to move some things aside to make room. I envisioned us snuggling in the dark. My head on his chest, listening to his heartbeat, feeling his chest rise as he took air in, and his breath—I imagined it being whisky-scented—making my hair flutter when he exhaled. In my imagination we lay there together, Grey and I. We took our last breaths together, there in the dark. No need for one to mourn the other, if we slipped away hand in hand, head on chest, heart to heart. I imagined it, sweet and soft.

And then the floor would be hard beneath me and the dust would choke me and Grey would be gone and the pain would be red in my eyes and I could see nothing else. It was dark. So dark.

And there wasn't even any whisky.

⁂

I LAY THERE a long, long time.

I close my eyes. Grey's chest rises and falls, his heart thum-thumping against my ear.

My eyes fly open. Jeriah will miss me when I'm gone. I weep as I imagined him receiving the news. *Your sister is dead.*

I can't do that to Riah. I'll make room for him here. *Grey, do you mind if I invite my brother to die with us?*

Of course I don't mind. It would be a kind gesture.

Riah climbs in and lies behind me. *Cozy.*

Oh, but now Seena will be bereft. I can't let her go through that.

Grey grunts. *Getting a little crowded in here, don't you think?*

The space widens to accommodate us.

Riah lifts his head and looks over me at Grey. *What's he doing here?*

Seena says, *Where are the children?*

Oh, yeah. The children. If I take their parents from them, they'll be orphans. Like me and Riah. I can't do that to KJ and Jeo.

Seena's gone.

Riah reaches across me to jab a finger at Grey. *Like I said. What's he doing here?*

He's my husband. I want him with me.

Well, then, you don't need me.

Riah's gone. And so is Grey. The floor is hard. The air is black. It stinks like an outhouse.

Why didn't I bring a flask?

⁂

AND STILL I lay there.

Sometimes I heard sounds. Thumping, grinding. Something resembling voices. Or maybe I just imagined it.

I managed to summon Grey from time to time, but my other companions never left me. Their names were Pain. Thirst. Hunger.

Grey sits across the table from me in the officer's lounge. I feel my hand in his—I quiver at his touch.

Or perhaps my other friends provoked that response. They're suddenly all I'm aware of. My heart races. *Grey, come back!*

His face comes into view, and I tremble all over. *Be careful, Jemma. I don't know what I'll do if anything happens to you.*

Poor, dear Grey. I wasn't careful enough.

I want to apologize. I want to say goodbye.

I LAY. STILL.

Cheek stuck to the floor. Crusty. Drool mixed with dirt? More likely tears.

Boom. Boom. Rumble. Everything shakes. More things falling. More dust.

Grey's chest rises and falls beneath me. His heart thum-thumps in my ear. It gets louder. The floor trembles. More dust.

I cough. I'm too thirsty to cough, but I can't stop coughing.

I WASN'T AWARE of it at the time, but later, I learned this:

The deadline for evacuation was up. Now that the City's people were out of the way, it was time to show Kentak what happens to traitors.

Wait! Grey's soul cried. *My wife hasn't been found!*

That's unfortunate. We're terribly sorry, but we can wait no longer. Justice must be swift.

A rain of bombs, a shower of missiles. Leave no structure standing—except, perhaps, the City installations. We'll leave those for last. A few of our people still search for survivors. Two more days, then the last brick will fall.

GREY WAS ENCAMPED outside Centre City with ten thousand other refugees housed in mobile emergency modules. He packed his bag, preparing to go AWOL, intending to make his way through the fiery terror to Suthfan to reach me. I was probably already dead, but he could no longer sit back and wait.

A knock startled him.

"Commander Standtall?" The voice was strained, but familiar. Grey opened the door.

A weary, stained, red-eyed Jeriah stood on the other side, barely standing. "I've been trying to get in touch with my sister. Is she here?" Riah paused long enough to assess the sight before his eyes. "Oh. She's not." He ran his filthy fingers through his hair. "Dripping, slimy slots."

Grey stepped back. "Jeriah. Come in and sit. You look ready to collapse."

The only place to sit was the bunk, and it was crowded with what few personal belongings Grey had managed to rescue from Yarapit.

Riah perched on the edge and pushed things back when they started to slide. "I'm sorry to bother you, sir, but I don't know what to do. I hoped she was with you." His voice broke.

Grey swallowed. "Jemma never got out of Arkentak."

Riah's head jerked up, his eyes wider than wide. "She what?"

"They didn't find her. She was in Suthfan. In one of the buildings that was hit. There were no survivors."

At Riah's agonized cry, Grey hastened to add, "I mean, they found no one alive, but none of the bodies were hers. They did not find her at all."

Riah hopped up and strode back and forth across the tiny cell. "Can't you do something? Slime, your slotting father is the Minister of Domestic Peace, for slot's sake. How can you not do something?"

"I am preparing to." Grey gestured at his half-packed bag. "I am going to look for her."

Riah sank back onto the bed. "No."

"What?"

"Don't do that."

"You said it yourself. How can I not do something? This is the only thing left to me."

Riah shook his head. "No, Commander."

"Do not call me that. In this situation, we are brothers."

Riah ran his hand down his face. "Okay, then. Ash. Or Grey. Or whatever you go by."

"Either or both, I do not care. But I am going. I must."

"No, you're not." Riah put both hands on his knees. "There's people there, looking. Right?"

Grey nodded.

"She didn't just vanish. If she's there, they'll find her. Right?"

"Presumably."

"Of course they will. And what happens if they find her alive? And you're dead because you were fool enough to try to get through the most massive air attack in City history? What happens if she's alive, but you're not?"

Grey sucked his lip. "But what if she's dead? Why shouldn't I join her?"

Riah lifted imploring, bloodshot eyes. "But what if she's not?"

⋇

I LIE THERE. Almost gone.

I try to form words, but my mouth is too dry. *Goodbye, Grey. There, I said it. Did you hear?*

Noises. Loud ones that shake the world, others less so. Crusty. Dusty. I cough.

What...? That was definitely a voice. Noises not far away. I cough again. Drat this dust, it hurts to cough.

"Hello?"

No, I'm just imagining voices. No one's there.

Lots of sounds. Movements. Voices. "I heard you cough. Can you hear me? Can you talk to me? I need to know where you are."

I try to call out, but I know they can't hear me. I can't even hear myself. I raise my good hand, try to make a fist. I pound on the panel above me. "Here!" I croak. A dying cricket would be louder. My pounding is a feather's touch, and the effort exhausts me. "Here!" My voice and tapping fade away, my energies spent forever.

"Guys! Over here!"

Lots of noise. Scrambling, talking. A beam of light blinds me and I scrunch my eyes tight.

"We've got a live one!"

❧ Chapter 9 ❧

WAKING TO HORROR

THEY DUG ME out. Stabilized me for moving. "I called for evac," a voice said.

Evac? This is a City installation. Shouldn't help already be here?

I felt stupid. Disconnected. Disoriented. Why was the air hazy with smoke? What were all those explosions? Why the whining and whoosh of projectiles? If something was wrong, shouldn't there be alarms going off?

"Notify her husband we found her."

No, he's here with me. Didn't you see him? Aren't you getting him out of that hole too?

They tore up my arm trying to insert an IV, thanks to my dehydrated veins and jarring from a nearby explosion. They threw themselves over me as debris pelted us.

"They know we're here, right?"

"I called, and they acknowledged. That one must have been off course."

"Slime, we gotta get out of here. They'll be razing this place before long."

What in the world are they talking about?

IV in. A short, noisy, earth-shuddering time later, sweet oblivion...

When I awoke, I wished I hadn't.

※

REGAINING CONSCIOUSNESS IN Walpin Rush Military Hospital in Centre City was a little like when I was a girl, awakening to find myself strapped to the bed in the hospital at Coldclime.

As before, Jeriah was there. His worried face was the first thing I saw when I opened my eyes. He sat in a chair to the left of the bed, leaning toward me.

I tried to say, "Hey," but my voice didn't work. I swallowed and tried again.

His eyes were weary, but a smile radiated relief to the rest of his face. "Welcome back."

"Back?" I croaked. "Where've I been?"

"Oh, just hiding under a collapsed building and scaring the slime out of us."

As he spoke, someone took hold of my hand on the other side. I turned my head.

"Grey!" I glanced back and forth between them. "You're together? In the same room?"

Grey had tears in his eyes, and I wanted to wipe them away. "You're back too, then. You were with me. Most of the time." I turned to Riah. "You were there a little while. Then Seena left so the kids wouldn't be alone, and you went after her. You didn't want to be there with Grey."

Riah and Grey exchanged glances.

"You remember, don't you? You were there, weren't you?" I asked first one, then the other.

Riah shook his head.

Grey squeezed my hand. That's when I realized my other arm, the one on Jeriah's side, was immobilized.

Grey said, "I *wanted* to be there."

I frowned. "No, you were there. I was—" I paused, wrestling with my memories. "Out of my mind." I let out a long breath. "Did I imagine it?" I gazed at Grey, drinking in the sight. The reality of his presence, the feel of his hand around mine.

He nodded. "I'm afraid so."

"It was a pretty nice imagining."

Still holding my hand, he half-rose to kiss me. "I wish I could have been there for real."

Riah stood. "I'll leave you two. I just wanted to make sure you were going to be okay."

I wanted to reach toward him, but my arm was immobilized. "No, don't go!" My voice was a croak.

He took my pinned-down hand. The two people I loved most in the world, each holding a hand. I didn't want the moment to end.

"I can't stay." His words hurt. "I'll be in big trouble if I don't get back soon. I've been waiting for two days for you to be fully conscious, and I can't stay any longer."

Fleeting memories came back to me. I had been awake before, hadn't I? I'd thought they were dreams, but no. I'd been drifting in and out. Doctors and nurses had been doing things to me. "Two days?"

He bent and kissed my forehead. "I can see you'll be fine now. You don't need me."

I tried to hold onto him, but he gently pulled out of my grip. "It's okay, Jem. You've got your pigeonhead." He crossed the room but stopped in the doorway and turned to face Grey. "You're going to tell her, Standtall. Before she sees it on the newsfeed." It was an order, not a question.

Tell me what? And why didn't Grey bristle at the way Jeriah spoke to him?

Instead of being angry, he nodded. "I'll tell her."

"Good. Do it." Jeriah stalked out.

"What's good? Do what?" I spoke to the doorway he'd just passed through. "Riah!"

"Shh, Freeman. It's okay." Grey's low voice was soft, reassuring, near my ear, his hand on my head. "You're safe. We're all safe now."

I breathed deeply against a rising panic. "Tell me what, Grey? What do I need to know?"

His hand still light and gentle on my head, he kissed my forehead—not my lips—and sank into his chair. "I'll tell you. But not today. Rest now, and I'll fill you in tomorrow."

I let out a long breath and felt I was sinking into the bed.

When I awoke again, it was dark outside the window, and Grey slept in the chair.

⁂

IT WASN'T UNTIL the next day that I learned how the world had changed while I was buried alive.

The information was delivered in the soft, raspy voice and the precise, careful speech of the man I loved. But the words he spoke were repugnant. Horrible. Beyond belief.

Before he was done, I hated the words. Hated the man who spoke them while he fingered the bracelet that bound me to him forever. He told me of the near-simultaneous missile attacks in not only Suthfan, but eleven other cities as well. Places I knew, like Damabal and Kenta City, as well as others I'd never visited, like Stamabal and Firkip. They left Yarapit alone. Apparently they didn't think it worth the bother.

He told me of the Kentans declaring their independence from the City. A declaration of war.

War against the City? What were they thinking? That their goddess Striden had commanded it, according to Grey's understanding. The goddess had somehow told them it was time to break the City's constraints, and she would give them victory.

He told me of the hasty retreat to protect City personnel from the onslaught to come.

Of the retribution even now being delivered to every urban area in the new nation of Kentak.

I tried not to imagine the deaths. The utter destruction. The people I'd known—my stylist in Damabal, the clerk in the liquor store in Yarapit, the front desk clerk at the hotel in Kenta City. All of them, they and their families, were now piles of mangled bones and ash. Or worse yet, not quite dead but dying in agony, or mourning their loved ones who lay buried in rubble.

I wanted to be sick, but my stomach was empty. I wanted to cry, and did.

He told me that after the hail of bombs and rain of fire came the snow of parachutes carrying LAST troops—the elite Land, Air and Sea Tactical soldiers, like Mayne—including Mayne, though of course Grey didn't know about him. They dropped into the areas where the Kentans had their underground bunkers. With specially developed laser drills, and using the detailed coordinates I and others in the Division had provided, they drilled through the ground into those bunkers. Through the holes they made, they dropped small canisters of a gas which, when exposed to air, burst into a flame that incinerated everything around and released corrosive fumes. If the people in the bunkers didn't die in the fire, their skin and lungs and airways would be eaten by the acid.

My sweet Mayne did this.

And I had provided some of the information that made it possible.

Worse yet, my grave, noble, and upright father-in-law commanded it.

But Grey wasn't finished. He then went on to tell me the City was drawing closed the net we'd laid for the collaborators in other parts of the world. All across the planet, many hundreds, including some CFCs, were arrested. When their interrogations were completed, they'd be executed.

Every vague prejudice that used to make me hate the Cityslimes was true after all. No, it was more than true. I'd never guessed how horrible they truly were. My former hatred had been based on legend and suspicion. The reality was worse. Far worse. My mind couldn't conceive of the horrors Grey was telling me.

"I want to see it," I said. "Where's the video controller? I want to see the newsfeeds."

Grey's voice was gravely, his face ashen and gray. "You don't want to see."

"Give me the controller. I want to see."

He rose, came around to the other side and opened a drawer of the bedside table. "You never watch television. You don't like the newsfeeds."

I snatched the controller out of his hand. "Give me that." I aimed it at the television and pressed the power button, but nothing happened. "What's wrong with this slotting thing?"

He pursed his lips. "You never watch television, so I didn't pay for the service. I can order it if you'd like."

"Order it? Haven't you ordered enough already?" Something rose within me, something terrible, something hateful. It hurt my chest. "Get out."

"What?"

"Get out. I hate you, Ashgrey Standtall. I never want to see your pigeon head again."

When he didn't move, I threw the controller at him.

He deflected it before it cracked him in the forehead. After a moment's consideration, he picked it up off the floor and handed it back to me. "I'll order the service. You may see it for yourself if you like." He bent, supporting himself on the bed rails, and spoke low and slow. "But do not blame me for what you see. You are as responsible as I."

The Thing within me started to growl deep in my throat. I felt it building, heard it coming, marveled at my powerlessness to stop it. It welled to a scream and came out sounding like, "Do you think I don't know that?"

Unfazed, he kissed my forehead. "I know you do."

He kissed my cheek. "If you didn't feel the way you do, I wouldn't love you so."

He kissed my lips. "This is difficult. For all of us. Very difficult."

He kissed me again. "But we'll get through it."

Another kiss. "However ugly the world is, I don't care. As long as we're in it together."

Two nurses appeared—male nurses who looked more like henchmen. "Information Officer Standtall, is everything okay?"

Oops, they'd heard my scream.

Grey unbent himself to stand tall. "Yes, gentlemen, thank you. We're all right."

They ignored him and looked at me, waiting for my response.

"No, it's not okay. I'd like television service in here, if you could. And this bed rail lowered so my husband can sit beside me."

⁂

THEY AGREED TO arrange for television service but were adamant about not allowing another person—not even my husband—in the bed with me. They did, however, bring a more comfortable chair for him.

We sat together and watched the reports.

It was worse than I had imagined. And I have a vivid imagination.

After a while Grey shut it off. "You've had enough."

I'd had more than enough.

"You need to sleep."

It was true, my eyes were heavy.

"I'll see you later."

I grabbed his hand. Put it to my face and ran the back of it across my cheek, then kissed it. "I'm sorry I yelled at you."

"I understand."

"I'm glad you do, because I don't. I don't understand anything anymore."

He kissed me. "You need time to digest things. You were buried in a hole for three days and on strong sedatives for two more. How could you not be confused?"

"Don't go until I fall asleep, okay?"

"Okay."

I don't think he had to wait more than a minute and a half. But the images of what I'd just seen filled my unconscious mind for the next several hours. I smelled the smoke. The burning buildings, burning flesh. I heard the screams of the dying.

But those images. One horrible picture after another chased through my dreams, blending into one another like molten plastic, like running blood.

I saw hands dropping a canister into a hole—they were Mayne's hands.

I saw the Minister of Domestic Peace standing by a window, holding a steaming cup and looking out on the world. The carpet was lush, the window tall, the drapery heavy and ornate. He looked out at the world and said, "Kill them. Kill them all." Then he took a sip of my uncle's glaffcrim.

Outside the window, the world exploded. But the Minister had turned away.

CITIZEN

❧ Chapter 10 ❧

THERAPY

I LIVED IN a fog. Someone was always poking, prodding, taking blood, putting me in one machine or another, running this test or that, covering my face with an anesthesia mask. For a week, I barely knew if I was awake or asleep, nor what was being done to me.

Grey was there sometimes, though I think not always. I don't believe I had any other visitors.

Nor did I want any. I only wanted to sleep and never wake up.

Grey told me the doctor was amazed I'd sustained so few internal injuries in connection with my fractured pelvis. I had some bleeding, but not enough to cause significant loss of blood or long-term damage.

My shoulder needed serious reconstruction, and it turned out to be rather complicated. But after a couple of surgeries, the orthopedic surgeon was satisfied I'd recover full use of my arm.

If not for the hopeful prognoses making Grey so happy, I wouldn't have cared. Bones would knit, wounds would heal, and drugs could relieve physical pain. But I needed something to ease my sorrow. So many had died. So many. Who was at fault? Was I? How could this horror be stopped? Who could save the world from itself?

I felt as if I were still buried in rubble. Even when Grey was with me, I was alone.

I'd been in the hospital ten days when the last person I wanted to see strode into my room: Dr. Pigeon. The original pigeonhead in full self-satisfied CFC plumage. At first I thought I was dreaming. But no, his cologne made my nose tickle. That wouldn't happen if it were a nightmare.

Though he was considerably older than Grey, his face was smooth like a mask. He must have had cosmetic surgery. "Well, well, well. You're awake." He picked up my chart and gave it a quick review.

I said nothing as he put it down and came near.

"How's my favorite patient?" He pulled out a penlight and checked my pupils. "Having a rough time of it, are we?"

I cleared my throat, as I seldom used it for speaking these days. "Wasn't too bad a day, till you came in."

He felt my face. "There's the Jemima I've loved for so long."

The idea of being loved by the Pigeon made me shiver.

My tremors made him frown. Or something did, anyway. He felt in his lab coat pocket, then rummaged in the drawer of my bedside table. Not finding what he was looking for, his frown deepened, and he buzzed the nurse's station.

No one answered.

I'd never seen the Pigeon so worked up. I used to try to rile him, but he never took the bait. Now, he bordered on livid, and I didn't know why. He strode into the hall and called, "I need a thermometer in here. Now!"

He waited in the doorway until someone brought one with a, "Here you are, Doctor."

I hadn't realized I'd dozed off again—I must have heard the thermometer exchange in my sleep—until I felt him press the instrument against the skin behind my ear, then again on my forehead. He swore like a Freemanslander. "When's the last time someone checked your temperature?"

"I don't know."

"You don't know? How can you not know?" He felt the glands in my neck. "Is that tender? Yes?"

All I could manage was a groan.

He reached beneath my shoulder binding to feel the glands in my armpit, and I winced.

He pulled off my covers then unwrapped my arm.

My shivering increased, but I was hot with embarrassment at the way he manhandled me. "What're you doing?" I tried to struggle but didn't make much headway.

"You have a high grade fever. I'm trying to determine the source of the infec—" He gasped. "Crying cornballs. What kind of a hospital is this?" He buzzed the nurses' station.

He got a prompt answer this time. "Is there a problem?"

The Pigeon's brand-new face was hard and red. "Yes, a big problem. This patient has blood poisoning."

"There must be some mistake. I'll notify her doctor. He's out of the hospital at present, but—"

"Yes, do. Notify him I am taking over the case. If we wait for him to get here, it could be too late."

⁂

ONCE THE INFECTION was discovered, it responded to treatment quickly. I hated it that the Pigeon had saved my life not once now, but twice. I'd rather have died than see him play the hero again.

Though he seemed to relish the role, he hadn't come to be my savior. He'd merely intended to tell me the results of some tests that I hadn't been aware had been done. That is, blood tests to check my level of trioxydiosmicoline stellase, the fancy name for worm juice. And brain scans, to see if the little critters had moved. Tests were run when I was first brought in, and again eight days later, to see if there was any change.

The results seemed anticlimactic by the time he had a chance to go over them with me, but here's what he'd been so eager to tell me when he arrived in my room that day: my stelli were still sleeping, but in a restless, sheets-tangled-around-the-legs sort of way.

The first blood test, drawn shortly after my arrival at the hospital, showed elevated levels of worm juice. The brain scan revealed the stelli had squirmed since my last scan a couple years before. That was the Pigeon's word. Squirmed. Apparently they hadn't moved from where they were lodged, but they'd changed their position in the bed, so to speak, excreting that trioxy-stuff as they rolled.

The level of worm juice in the second blood test was nearly back to where it had been before the explosion, and the second scan showed no further movement.

"They must have begun to stir in the stress of your situation," the Pigeon said. "But it appears they are returning to their dormant state." He almost sounded disappointed. "We shall do a blood test every two days while you're here to monitor the situation."

He stood at the foot of my bed in his immaculate CFC attire. Beside him, Grey stood three or four inches taller, his rebellious forelock a limp squiggle above his heavy brow and his deep, dark eyes glistening with worry. "What does it mean? Are they likely to stay quiet now?"

At the same time, I asked, "You didn't put me on that Kaemasine stuff again, did you? I hate that stuff. It makes me crazy."

"Of course I did," the doctor said.

"What stuff?" Grey asked.

"Kaemasine," Pigeon said. "It's the standard treatment for preventing the dormant stelli from awakening."

Grey's eyes widened. "There's a way to do that?"

"Yes," the doctor answered at the same time as I said, "No."

I hurried up and explained before the Pigeon could get in a squawk. "It's the standard treatment, but it doesn't work. Stelli always wake up sooner or later, but I've been off the treatment for a decade without anything happening. Until now. So I don't figure the drug does anything except make me angry and depressed."

Pigeon put on his doctor-knows-best face. "Now, Jemima—"

Grey held up his hand to stop the flow of nonsense. "Is that true? It caused depression when she was on it before?"

"Possibly, but she was—"

"She hasn't been taking anything since I've known her. It's really been ten years since she stopped the treatment? And nothing's happened in all that time?"

Pigeon frowned. "Yes. But since they started to stir, I had no choice but to put her back on it."

"I agree. Now that the blood levels are normal again, though, I think you should take her off the drugs and see what happens. She has enough to be depressed about. I'd rather she not have drugs that make it worse."

Pigeon took a deep breath. "With all due respect, Commander, you're not a physician. I've studied stellasedes my entire career, and no one knows the condition better than I. You are hardly in a position—"

I might have spoken a little louder than necessary—blame the Kaemasine—but I had to interrupt. "You're wrong, Pigeon. *I* know the condition better than you. Do you have worms in your head? No. Did you grow up on a drug that made you feel like there's a fuzzy weight pressing down on you and you can't throw it off, and all you want to do is dig a hole and hide in it and knock down anyone who gets in your way? I didn't think so. Because if you did, you'd rather die than live like that again."

The doctor and Grey both gaped at me. I guess I was shouting. I might even have been thrashing around in the bed, as much as I could with a broken pelvis and shoulder.

Pigeon just stood there, but Grey was by my side in an instant, trying to calm me. I don't remember what he did, what he said, I was so worked up, so drugged up. I remember getting mad and yelling, and I remember Grey insisting the Kaemasine be discontinued, and Pigeon finally agreeing. But the memory is a blur.

After the Kaesamine was discontinued, my mood gradually changed. But I still had a heaviness in my chest not related to any physical injuries. Though I couldn't put a name to it, it seemed tangible enough to show up in a CT scan. But it didn't.

If I believed in such things, I might have thought my soul was torn.

⁂

IT'S NEVER GOOD to lie around on a broken pelvis. But with an injured shoulder, I couldn't use a walker or crutches.

For therapy sessions, they surrounded my midsection with a brace that suspended me from above. In that contraption I was able to walk a little, with the brace holding some of my weight and the therapist providing stability. It was an awkward arrangement, to say the least, and the brace rubbed me sore every place it touched. But I worked at it diligently, trying to gain mobility and be released as soon as possible. I hoped freedom from this hated hospital might help my emotional recovery.

I lay on my bed following a painful, exhausting session when unfamiliar sounds arose in the hall. Important Person sounds. As if a security team was locking down the floor.

I stared toward the doorway. Official-sounding voices, doors closing, feet thumping in determined step. I caught a glimpse of uniforms passing. Ministry Security.

What was going on? Why would the City secure my hospital floor?

Two Ministry Security men stepped in and took positions on either side of the doorway. Two more entered. After closing the drapes, they inspected the room, leaving no drawer unopened. They paid no attention to me whatsoever, except when one of them looked under the bed with a curt, "Excuse me, ma'am" before bending down.

I said nothing. Just watched in confusion.

One of them spoke into a device, "Clear to enter," and more footsteps clipped down the hall. I watched the doorway with a dull sort of curiosity.

Three people entered—two more security men, followed by my father-in-law.

"Oh!" The exclamation popped out of my mouth without thought. "Minister Standtall." I felt I should stand, but couldn't.

He spoke to the men with him. "Leave us."

They nodded and filed out, taking up positions outside the room.

He closed the door, then turned his deep, dark gaze to me. His weary eyes were sunken, his face lined and pale. "Jemima, my dear."

Why was he here? What did he want from me? I needed Grey with me. "Sir?"

"I apologize for the ridiculous show." He gestured toward the door. "All the Council is under tight security. It is inconvenient, but perhaps less so than assassination would be."

"I suppose that's true, sir."

He hesitated a moment, then put his hand on the back of the chair across the room. "May I?" He motioned toward the bed as if asking if he could bring the chair near.

He asked *me* for permission? "Of course."

He moved it near, then sat. "I am sorry about all this, Jemima."

Yeah. So am I. I didn't answer. Just nodded.

He pursed his lips. "I am not sure we can— No, I am sure. We cannot truly understand each other. But if you permit, I would like—" He sounded like Grey when he was flustered. "Will you endure the ramblings of a weary old man?"

He did look old. He seemed to have aged ten years in the few months since I'd last seen him.

Not waiting for my reply, he continued. "You receive counseling in addition to care for your bodily injuries?"

"I can't be discharged unless I do. I'll put up with just about anything if it will get me out of here."

He pursed his lips. "The counseling is not helpful?"

It wasn't, but I didn't want to sound bitter. "It's probably too soon to say."

"I feel in need of counsel myself, and I hope you might help me."

"I don't see how, sir. My thoughts are of no consequence."

"Not so." He placed his hands on his knees. "You are my daughter-in-law. Not only that, but you are a worthy person in your own right, not merely because my son loves you." He paused. "Which he does, very much. Very much indeed."

"He does." My eyes filled, and the weakness irritated me. I cleared my throat. "I'm amazed by that every day."

His face softened, just a little. "Love is inexplicable. But his mother and I are more pleased than we can express that he chose you. Even more, that you are alive after this ordeal."

"Thank you, sir."

He let out a long sigh. "I deserve no thanks. Your troubles are my fault."

My eyes widened. "It was a Kentan blast that got me, not one of ours."

I guessed his answer before he gave it. "As the one responsible for keeping the peace of the City, the present situation is my personal failure."

"Sir, that's—"

He lifted a hand. "I speak nonsense. Just an old man's ramblings." He leaned forward. "But it is sincere nonsense. I am not legally responsible. My conscience is clear on that count. But is law the only glue that holds the world together?"

Before I could offer an answer, he continued. "I speak of moral responsibility. I should have stopped this before it began. That was my duty. To assure the City's peace, as my predecessors have done from the beginning. Never before has war marred City tranquility."

I shifted my weight and winced at the pain in my bones, in his words. "The uprising was in the making long before that duty was yours. There has always been resentment against the City, deep and widespread. What can one man do in the face of that?"

"I am not one man. I am the City, with eyes everywhere, and arms, and feet. It is my job to see. To know. To act."

His dark, red-rimmed eyes lit on my bandaged shoulder. "I ignored a localized infection, allowing it to spread throughout the whole world. Now we fight a poison in our very blood."

Though I wanted to blame him—I needed *someone* to blame—I knew he was wrong. Deep down, I knew this wasn't his fault. But I couldn't put words to that knowledge. "I believe there's more to it than that, sir."

"Oh?" He waited for me to continue.

I fingered my thoughts, trying to arrange them into an explainable shape. "That poison? It's been there for a lifetime or more, but it was quiet. Building strength before bursting out. It's like—like a stellas worm."

His brows arched like question marks. "Like a what?"

"A Freemanslandian brain worm. You know, the parasites that make us go crazy?"

"I thought that was a myth."

Grey had never told his parents I was infected? "The stellas worms are real, but I suppose the stories are exaggerated. The wild people of the woods, half-human and half-beast? The wraiths and haunts? Those are just tales." I suppressed a shudder at the memory of the stellasedes I'd seen in the wild as a girl. There was a horrible truth behind the mythology. "But my point is, the worms embed themselves in a person's brain and lie dormant. You never know when they're going to wake up. In the meantime, the infected person looks and acts like anyone else."

His expression was thoughtful, but he didn't interrupt as I went on.

"That disease you spoke of has lain dormant for decades. This wormy world was living normally until now, but it was always infected."

He pursed his lips. "What makes you say that?"

I'm not sure what emboldened me. Perhaps it was that he'd been so jarringly open with me. Or because he reminded me so much of Grey. For whatever reason, I spoke my mind to one of the most powerful men in the world. "Growing up on Freemansland, I hated the City for taking over our island. We had our own ways, and we resented the City's interference. That hatred ran deep everywhere on Freemansland, though perhaps less so on the third level, the one we call Coldclime. That's where the City's presence is strongest, where the government offices, the hospital, the City schools are located. As a result, a few of the people who live there have come to see that the changes made by the City have improved their lives, not hurt them. But most of Freemansland is like I was. They believe the City is horribly evil. And in my travels, I've found much of the rest of the world shares that opinion."

He shook his gray head. "I had no idea so many resented us."

"I'm sure you didn't. People treat you with respect everywhere you go because they're afraid of you."

"I suppose that is so." He didn't seem to like the thought. "But we have bettered the life of every individual in the world. What is there to resent? Should not the world be grateful?"

"How would you like someone barging into your home, tearing everything up, rebuilding it to suit themselves, and insisting you should like it?"

"That does not describe what the City has done." He frowned. "Our actions have always been those of compassion. We brought deliverance from poverty and disease. We offered help and hope to a world that had none." His sigh was long and heartfelt. "But some rebel nevertheless. It is such a terrible sorrow. I grieve much like a father who must regretfully punish his child. A terrible punishment multiplied by millions." He sagged in his chair. "The rebellion in Kentak is crushed, yes. But in the process, so am I."

Perhaps. But next moment, he sat upright and composed his face. "Do you resent us still? If so, why did you marry my son?"

Though his voice was calm, his eye was sharp. I didn't doubt he was grieved, but he was in no way crushed.

"I'm not sure how I feel about the City these days. I went from rabid, frothing hatred to jaw-clenching endurance to grudging admiration. And then I met Ashgrey. And I didn't care who he was. I married him for one reason. To be with the man I loved."

His expression relaxed. "I knew that. I wasn't aware of the rabid, frothing hatred and jaw-clenching endurance." He almost smiled. "You have a way with words. But from our first meeting, I could see that you love my son the man and are not impressed by his name. Most see his status and look no further. But you are clearly different." He leaned back and studied me. "I do not believe, however, that I have ever before met a person who hated the City."

"I'm pretty sure you have, sir. You just weren't aware of it. Much as you can't tell a person has brain worms by looking at him."

I met his gaze, and those glittering eyes locked into mine for a terrifying moment as if he was reading my mind. Or seeing my brain worms.

If he saw them, he didn't flinch. Instead, he rose. "I apologize for interrupting your rest. I can see you are weary."

"I was. But your visit has energized me."

"I am glad of that. On my part, I find your words better than a shot of strong crim after a sleepless night." He put the chair back where he'd found it. "What might I do to assist your recovery?"

I started to say, "Nothing," but another thought tumbled from my mouth without warning. "I'd like to go swimming."

One brow rose, and he cocked his head as if to get a better view of this strange creature before him. "Swimming."

"Yes, sir. I think it would be more effective therapy than what they're having me do now. It would take the weight off my pelvic bones while allowing me to exercise every muscle. Until I have range of motion in my shoulder, I can swim one-handed, no problem." I paused, remembering our honeymoon at Quarry House, and smiled a little. "Ashgrey says I'm a fish."

His head tipped the other direction. "I see what you're saying." He straightened. "I will arrange it."

Just like that? Not, *I'll see what I can do,* or *Perhaps we can come up with a plan?* He sounded as if he already had a plan. I tried not to gape like the Freemansland fish that I was. "Thank you, sir."

He took my good hand, bent and kissed it, then gave me a tired smile. "Thank *you,* my dear. Our talk has been my therapy today."

I didn't see how it could have helped him. But I wasn't lying when I said his visit did me good.

I still couldn't grasp all that was wrong with the world. But it was heartening to see my father-in-law was not the enemy. He was still Grey's dear papa.

Not a terrible man, but man with a terrible responsibility.

104

❧ Chapter 11 ❧

RECOVERY

LEFT ARM IMMOBILIZED, I hung onto the pool's rail with my right hand and, with Grey's assistance, eased myself into the water. My therapist, Naka, stood ready to help.

I'd wanted to just flop in off the side, but Grey and Naka both discouraged it.

"It's best to take it slow at first," Naka had advised.

Grey shook his head. "I know you're a fish, but you've only got one flipper."

I scowled. "Fish don't have flippers." But I didn't press the issue. I was just glad to be in my element again.

When Minister Standtall said he'd arrange a swim for me, his mind had made a quick leap far beyond the simple water therapy I'd been thinking of. A week after his visit, I was bundled into a medical transport and carried away to Sentinel Pines along with Naka as my personal therapist and two nurses, Kippie and Renna. We were met by Dr. Genley, the Standtalls' family physician, and the estate steward, Starham, who took us to the suite my in-laws had prepared for me.

It was part clinic, part apartment. We entered a drawing room. Attached to that was an exam/treatment room, an office, and a lab for processing the blood samples Dr. Pigeon still required be drawn on a regular basis. I had a personal suite consisting of a bedroom—including the requisite massive closet—a handicapped-accessible bathroom, and a dining area, all roomier than anyone could possibly need. The nurses and Naka had a suite as well, though I wasn't given a tour of it.

Starham explained the house rules. As family, I was to have the use of every amenity on the estate. One of those was the indoor pool, which was designated for the exclusive use of my physical therapy at certain times each day.

As employees, my attendants had restricted access. They could use the pool, but only during specified hours. Starham handed them a booklet detailing the rules.

Something in me wanted to object. I shouldn't be singled out for special treatment. Nor did I need two nurses and a therapist who had nothing to do but take care of me.

I might have argued against my moving there, but two things stopped me. For one, my caregivers were clearly delighted with the situation. Restricted access notwithstanding, they took one look at the layout, and you'd have thought they were schoolgirls on a holiday.

Mostly, though, was the fact that Grey would share the suite with me. He would be gone during the day and some evenings, but when he came home, that would be the home he came to.

He'd told me this the last time he visited me in the hospital. My gaze took in his chiseled face, his broad shoulders, his long legs as he sat in the chair beside my bed. "You mean you'll be in the same house?"

"I mean I'll be in the same suite."

"As in, the same apartment?"

His eyes crinkled in that dear, near-smile of his. "As in, the same bedroom. Do you have a problem with that?"

I tried to keep my own grin at bay. "I might have a physical problem with that, but we'll work through it."

He wasn't there when we arrived, but he came in that evening as Naka and I ate dinner in my suite.

I liked Naka, both as a therapist and as a person, not only because she shared the name of one of the few friends I had in the IA. When I learned Naka Nutt died in Dabamal the same day I'd almost died in Suthfan, it hit me hard. I think I transferred some of my fondness for my friend onto my therapist.

Or maybe I just liked her.

She ate with me that evening for professional reasons, but I was glad of her company. I'd just told her about an incident in a session with a therapist at the hospital, and we laughed about it until the door buzzer alerted us that someone had entered the suite.

Naka and I paused and exchanged glances. This wasn't a real clinic, so no one expected strangers to walk in. Then I said, "Oh, I'll bet that's my husband."

"I'm sure that's it." Naka rose. "I'm through eating anyway, so I'll get out of the way."

"No, don't. You can't leave that good fish on the plate. At least stay until you've finished it."

She shook her head. "I'm full. Really, I—"

Grey appeared in the doorway, and my heart fluttered at the sight of him.

He nodded to Naka. "Please, don't let me interrupt."

"Hello, Commander." She cleared her place and set the dishes on the sideboard. "Have you eaten? I can call the kitchen and—"

He held up a hand. "Already taken care of. But I don't want to chase you from your dinner."

Naka blushed. "That's okay, sir. I'm through, really I am. Are you sure I can't get you anything before I leave?"

"I'm certain." He stood tall and straight and so compelling that poor Naka seemed about to lose her composure entirely.

She flashed me a quick smile. "I'll see you tomorrow, then. Nine o'clock. Good evening."

And then she was gone, leaving me alone with Grey in our own apartment.

It had been a long time.

He pulled out the chair beside me.

"Before you sit—" I gestured toward the sideboard. "Would you mind bringing me that piece of fish she left? No point letting it go to waste."

⁂

WHATEVER PHYSICAL problems I experienced that night, we worked through them.

⁂

ONE OF THE PHYSICAL problems I had the next morning was trying to put on a swimsuit for my first water therapy session.

Grey had requested the day off to get me settled in, and I was happy to have him, rather than one of the nurses, assist with my wardrobe issues.

Once my suit was on without rolls or twists, I watched him change into his own.

I approved of what I saw. "You've been working out."

"Yes, I have."

"I've been thinking for awhile that you looked different, but my brain's been so fuzzy, I couldn't be sure."

He slipped on a robe. "Are we ready?"

"I am. Can't speak for you."

"Don't I look ready?"

"You look ready for anything. Is the Division on some sort of fitness kick all of a sudden?" They had always required us to stay in shape, but it seemed he'd been putting more effort into it than usual.

He helped me into my wheelchair. "No, it's my decision. I'm training again."

"Training." It wasn't a question. "For pugilism."

He wheeled me out of the bedroom. "What else? You swim, I pugil."

"Swimming seems much more civilized. Which is strange, since it's I who am the barbarian."

"Pugilism is civilized. There are strict rules, limitations. We don't pummel one another to the death."

"I know that. And I know you used to be good at it. But you're getting a little old for that sort of thing, don't you think?"

"I'm not training to compete, just to get into shape." He bent to speak softly in my ear as we neared the drawing room where Naka waited. "And work out some of my frustration."

"Frustration?" I craned my head to look up at him. "Even after last night?"

He chuckled. "Okay, less so now. But that's not what I meant."

I wasn't sure what he meant but figured it had to do with the war. With almost losing me. The shock of seeing the authority of the City Fathers challenged and the horrific vehemence of their response.

How much of that retaliation was he a part of? I was on the outside now, knowing only what I saw on the newsfeed.

"I understand," I said. But I didn't. For me, the war was over. My only mission now was to recover.

⁂

FOR RECOVERY PURPOSES, my time at Sentinel Pines was productive and mostly enjoyable.

The Pigeon remained in charge of my case for a few more weeks, as he wasn't willing to step back and let Dr. Etsiben take over. I'd been assigned to Etsiben from the time I was brought into the hospital, but he had no experience with stellasedes. I imagine he was relieved to be relieved of me.

Fortunately, the Pigeon wasn't a hummingbird and didn't hover. When he came by after a week to check on me, he declared me sufficiently improved that I no longer needed the two nurses. For once, he and I agreed on something. I never thought I needed a nurse to begin with, let alone two. After they left, it was just Naka and me—or Grey and me, when he was home—with Dr. Genley on call in case of emergency.

We never had to call him.

The Pigeon flew in again after a month. He did a physical exam and checked my blood himself. He and said my worms were sleeping soundly, and unless he had reason to suspect a change, he wouldn't bother me for another half a year.

At six weeks, I went back to the hospital to be checked by the surgeons who had worked on my pelvis and shoulder. At eight weeks, after a final check-up, I was officially released from their care.

At that point, Dr. Etsiben examined me on behalf of the Division to determine if I was fit to serve.

"You've made excellent progress. That swim therapy was a marvelous idea. You're fortunate to have a family who could make that happen. I'd prescribe it for others if we had the facilities for it here."

I nodded. "I've always been a swimmer."

"It's served you well." He'd been studying something on his tablet as he spoke, but now he lifted his head and gave me his full attention. "You'll have served your ten years next month. Do you plan to re-up?"

I'm not sure why I hesitated, because leaving after ten years had always been my plan. But everything was different now. I was different. The world was different. The City needed people with my skills. Was it right for me to leave?

Before I was injured, Grey had been in favor of my retirement. If his opinion had changed, he'd never mentioned it. He must be assuming I'd go ahead with the original plan.

"No," I told the doctor. "I'll retire."

He nodded. "That's probably best. I'm okaying you for duty until your term's up, but on medical restriction. You'll probably be assigned to a desk somewhere here in Centre City, and then you'll be discharged as a Citizen of Merit." He slipped his tablet in his pocket. "You'll have some shoulder pain for a while, and your hips are likely to ache for another few months. But by this time next year, you'll be in fine shape, pursuing whatever life you choose as a citizen of the City."

He stood and extended his hand. "I wish you the best."

I rose too—without assistance—and shook his hand. "Thank you, doctor." But one phrase in his last sentence stuck in my head like a brain worm. *Pursuing whatever life you choose.*

I had no idea what that might be.

❧ Chapter 12 ❧

HOME

"HERE WE ARE." With almost child-like excitement, Grey unlocked the door. "Home at last."

While I recovered at Sentinel Pines, Grey had purchased an apartment for us in the River Park area. He took care to furnish and decorate it without my help, giving no hints as to what it was like. He only promised that I'd approve.

I entered, as eager as he.

I'd felt a little like a trespasser at Sentinel Pines, even though Mimma went out of her way to make me welcome. She sometimes had me join her for meals, for rounds of her favorite board game, Okolo, or just to sit and chat, either in my suite or elsewhere in the house. No matter what, she was always delightful company. But she traveled more often than she was home, and I was usually left to rattle around the huge place without her. I couldn't consider it home.

The place to which Grey now brought me was *our* home.

Only a CFC can own property. Under City law, even Uncle Rhe was merely the tenant and caretaker of his family's ancestral plantation, not its actual owner. But Grey and I owned the building we stood in—he by birthright, I by marriage.

He opened the door and ushered me in with a wide sweep of his arm. "What do you think?"

The marble-floored foyer, small and tasteful, had only a table, a mirror, a chair, and a closet. The latter contained empty hangers—for guests' coats, as ours hung in another closet—and an umbrella. Yes, I looked. I peeked into every corner, as Grey watched with a proud smile.

Beyond the arched doorway, the Standtall-sized sitting room was furnished in classic Durbin-Kynah style, solid and graceful and upholstered to the hilt. Grey crossed the room and opened the heavy drapes, revealing a stunning view of the city from our twenty-first-floor vantage point.

I could describe everything in detail—the hardwood floor, the high ceiling, the light fixtures—but I'll skip all that and go to the far wall, which is where my attention first went. Three-quarters of the expanse, from the wainscoting almost to the ceiling, was an aquarium.

I headed toward it. "Glish, look at that!"

Grey laughed. "Do you like it?"

"I've never seen anything like it." Most of the fish species were familiar sights in the stillwaters of Freemansland. I recognized the plants as well. And rising up from the center of the tank glimmered a miniature model of the island, lit from above. It was hollow, and the tank's creatures were able to swim in and out of it.

Standing behind me, Grey wrapped his arms around me and nuzzled my neck. "But do you like it?"

I shook my head. "No."

He froze. "No?"

"No." I turned to face him. "I absolutely love it."

I could have studied the aquarium for hours, but eventually he pulled me away to show me the rest of the apartment.

Everything I put my eye and hand on was quality, but in a casual, understated way. It was the sort of place a Standtall could be proud of but a Freeman could be comfortable in—and that was no small feat.

The master bedroom was appropriately massive, with his-and-hers closets big enough to house a family of four. The two guest rooms each had their own bathrooms. Besides the usual dining room, media room, and office, Grey had added a weight room with exercise equipment.

I surveyed the very Grey-ness of the gym and pretended to disapprove. "What, no swimming pool?"

"There's a competition-sized pool in the basement level for the use of all the tenants. I already showed it to you."

"There's a weight room down there, too. So why do you need this one?"

He shrugged. "I thought it would be nice to have one of my own."

"Fine with me." I ran my hand along his bicep. "It'll be easier for me to watch you get all sweaty."

The whole apartment, not just the weight room, reflected Grey's tastes. He was no doubt aware of it, which is probably why he made sure to include the aquarium for me. But I wouldn't have changed a thing.

And then there was the kitchen. He seemed to take special pleasure in pointing out its many useful features.

"Lovely," I finally said, "but it's a little more than I need, don't you think?" I ran my hand across the big, intimidating stove, with its dials, buttons, and burners. "Ten years from now, this will look as new as it does today. The only thing I can make is glaffcrim."

"Oh, but you can learn. You have time now."

I blinked up at him. What was he suggesting?

"Now that you're not working for the IA, I mean. You have the time for it." He patted his firm, flat belly. "To feed your poor hungry husband."

I struggled to follow his logic. "There's every kind of restaurant known to mankind within a few kilometers of here, and they all offer delivery. Why should anyone cook?"

"Lots of reasons." He ticked them off on his long fingers, starting with his thumb. "So you can use this nice kitchen." First finger. "To fend off boredom. I know you've been wondering what to do with yourself once you retire."

That much was true. But learning to cook had never crossed my mind, and it didn't appeal now.

Grey raised a third finger. "It's a creative outlet. You're the creative type, so you'll enjoy it."

Cooking, a creative outlet? I'd always thought it must be a chore.

He continued the count. "It's something new to explore, and you love a challenge. And let's not forget the main reason." He splayed all five fingers. "To please your husband. Because you love me." His hand sank and his expression turned pensive. "You do love me, don't you?"

I pursed my lips, pretending to think about it. "Well, sure, I suppose I do, a little." Gazing into those deep, glaffcrim eyes, I couldn't keep the smile from my lips. "Maybe more than a little." I put my arms around his neck, ignoring the twinge in my left shoulder. "Would my learning to cook really make you happy?"

He kissed me. "Yes, it would." He put his hands on my hips and pulled me close.

"Why?" I asked his neck.

He was too busy kissing my ear, my neck, my shoulder, to answer right away, but finally began, "So you can..." and between kisses, completed the sentence, "... impress... my parents... when they visit... next month."

I pulled away. "Impress who when they what? Your parents? Here? I'm supposed to cook for them?"

He took my face in gentle hands. "It's okay, you don't have to. As you said, we can always order something. But they'd both be so proud of you if you made dinner yourself. It's what a wife does."

I knew that. Despite having servants at their disposal, all the women in Grey's family took pride in cooking for their husbands from time to time. I'd heard them talking about it.

"Well..." I leaned into him. "It's true, I do like a challenge...."

THOUGH GREY WANTED me to cook, he nixed the idea of my doing the housecleaning. "It's not appropriate."

"You didn't have a problem with me keeping our apartment clean in Yarapit."

"That was a completely different situation." His jaw was firm, determined.

"Why? You like a clean house. I have more time now than I did then, and I don't mind doing it. What's the big deal?"

His heavy brows grew heavier. "I let you do it then because we didn't have a choice. Your having to clean it was just one of the many things I hated about that place, and I'd rather you never mentioned that horrible flat again. We live here now. This is *our* house, and you're my wife, not my servant."

It was a class thing, apparently, and I still hadn't learned all there was to know about being a CFC. "So it's not servile to cook, just to clean? Who makes these rules?"

He tipped his head as if he'd never considered the question. "There aren't rules. That's just the way it is."

"If there's no rulebook, how can I learn what's appropriate and what isn't?"

"You already know, mostly."

That was our second day in our new home, and we sat at the table after supper—a meal that had been delivered by a local restaurant, as I hadn't yet started my cooking classes. I gathered the plates to take them into the kitchen. "Am I permitted to clear the table and put the things in the dishwasher? Or do I have to save everything for the housekeeping team?"

He tapped his fingers on the table. "Don't get smart with me. You know how it works."

I set the plates back on the table, perhaps a little harder than necessary. "No, I don't know, Grey. I'm still trying to figure all these things out. In the IA, when they prepared me for an assignment, they taught me everything I needed to know about the culture I'd be living in. But now, I'm suddenly a civilian citizen living in Centre City, but I don't know what I'm supposed to do. If you don't teach me, I'm going to embarrass you in front of your parents."

The tension crease between his brows smoothed in an instant. "I'm sorry. You're so good at whatever you do, I forget you don't know everything. Of course I'll help you learn."

And he did. We practiced the visit, from greeting his parents at the door, to showing them the house, to serving the meal, to clearing the table, so I could be comfortable with the whole process.

"How many bodyguards are they going to have with them?" I asked. "Will I feed them too?"

He shook his head. "The guards will do a sweep of the place, then go out in the hall to wait. You only have to make dinner for the four of us."

I soon learned he was only partly right.

A week before their visit, the Minister's security team requested a menu and a list of every ingredient I would be using, right down to the salt and pepper. And they insisted on providing all the supplies to "ensure it was all of the best quality." That's what they said, but Grey and I both knew it was a precaution against poisoning.

When I told them I would make the soup the day before, a guard brought me the ingredients, watched while I made it, then took it with him when it was finished. Early in the day of the visit, they returned the soup so I could reheat and serve it on schedule—but only after inspecting every pan, utensil, and plate, and removing everything from my cabinets and refrigerator I wouldn't be using for the meal.

After performing a final inspection of the house, however, they waited in the hall during the visit, as Grey had promised.

He and I showed his parents the place, and they expressed their approval of everything they saw—especially, in Mimma's case, the aquarium. Then Grey had them take their seats in the dining room.

He helped me serve, beginning with a simple green salad followed by vutroi soup. I served glazed sabrefish steaks as an entree, with baked kartroots and a thin legumash on the side. I rounded out the meal with peach ice cream for dessert. And, of course, there was a different wine with each course.

It all went smoothly. Grey exuded pride the whole evening, and I reveled in it. Maybe I'd be able to pull off this CFC charade.

Could it be that it wasn't a charade?

As we sipped our after-dinner crim in the sitting room, Mimma remarked again on the aquarium. "It is such an unusual addition to the decor, and the fish do not seem to be the usual tropical fish. Whatever gave Ashgrey the idea?"

"He wanted me to feel at home here. Most of the fish are native to Freemansland, like me. He took great pains to choose varieties I'd recognize and that could live in the same tank without eating each other."

She gazed into the water. "That tower-like object. Is that a tiny model of the island of Freemansland?"

I nodded. "That's correct."

"What a strange place. What part did you live on?"

I pointed to the second layer. "I was born here, on the level called Freedom. When my brother and I were about ten years old, we were made wards of the City. That's when we went to live with our aunt and uncle on their glaffcrim plantation on the third level, Glaffit."

"Oh?" She turned to me, brows raised. "I thought you always lived with them."

I shook my head. "No, ma'am. I was born on Freedom."

Grey and his father turned their attention our way about then. The Minister took a sip of crim. "How did you come to be wards of the City? Were you suddenly orphaned?"

Suddenly orphaned. No, I was born an orphan. But that would be too hard to explain.

On the other hand, I liked these people. I thought I might even love them. I shouldn't keep secrets from them.

"I was born on Freedom," I repeated. "My brother and me. We were twins. My mother died delivering me. My father blamed me for killing her."

The Minister's eyes widened, and Mimma gasped.

"Or at least, that's what I was told. When I was much older, my aunt told me my father wanted to kill me for causing my mother to die. Apparently he loved her, though I can't imagine him loving anyone. He certainly didn't love me. My grandmother hid me from him. She was afraid he'd kill both us babies in his drunken fury, so she took my brother and me and went up to Glaffit, to my Aunt Lanie. Gran carried us on her back, climbing up the whole long stairway to the next level, because she didn't have money for the scaler fare."

Mimma looked puzzled. "The scaler?"

I explained about the vehicle that climbed up and down the sharpfall and the stairway that could be used in a pinch.

I continued my story. "She got to the top, and it was raining, and she was exhausted from carrying the two of us up almost four hundred steep steps, and someone saw her and asked where she was going. 'To Moll,' she said, and the kind stranger took her across the stillwater on his boat and dropped her off at the dock. She had to climb another stairway to get to the plantation halfway up the next sharpfall."

Mimma covered her mouth with bejeweled hands. "That poor lady!"

"Aunt Lanie and Uncle Rhe had only been married a few months and they really didn't want twin babies to raise, but when Gran showed up with the two of us, they couldn't very well say no. Gran stayed for a couple of days, then went back down to Freedom without us.

"After a few weeks, our father quit drinking long enough to remember he had a newborn son. When Gran told him what she'd done, he went up to Moll and demanded his son back. Took Jeriah back and left me with Aunt Lanie.

"But then she got pregnant and had my cousin, Daree. And Daree was unhealthy at first, and fussy, and Aunt Lanie was getting worn down trying to keep up with a one-year-old and a sick newborn, and help with the crim business too. So Uncle Rhe sent word down to Gran and Papa that they'd have to take me back."

Tears filled Mimma's eyes, and I spoke faster. "So I went back. And I stayed there with Gran and Jeriah until my father died." Okay, so maybe I wouldn't tell them every detail. "By then, Gran was—" I glanced over at Grey, wordlessly asking how much I should divulge.

"Her grandmother wasn't well," he finished for me. Not, *she was a stellasede, and the worms were moving,* which was what I'd been going to say.

"Yes," I said. "We were orphans, and that's why we were made wards of the City."

Mimma patted my hand. "Oh, my dear, that is so very sad. What a terrible time that must have been." Then she gave my hand a squeeze. "I am happy I can be your Mimma now."

"So am I," I said. And I meant it.

"And I hope you know that we love you like a daughter."

Across the room, the Minister nodded. "We do indeed. Can I infer that your unusual childhood is the source of those stories you tell our grandchildren?"

I shrugged. "Some of them. Others, I just make up."

He set down his cup. "You are a gifted storyteller. Have you ever thought of going into it professionally?"

"A professional storyteller, sir?" I'd heard of such things, but I wasn't cut out for the performing arts.

"Or a writer. Of children's books. I think you have a gift for it."

"I—I'd never given it a thought, sir."

Mimma clapped. "I think it's a wonderful idea! Do consider it, won't you?"

"I will," I said. "I'll consider it." But I didn't promise to consider it seriously. Me? Write children's stories? I didn't even like children.

⁂

MY IN-LAWS' VISIT marked the beginning of the holiday season.

First Day has always been the brightest date on the City calendar, with more celebrations spiraling out from it than tornados spawned by a hurricane. But after the Kentak Rebellion, the City Fathers ramped everything up even more to remind the world what a wonderful thing it was to be part of the global Centre City family. Travel, parties, and various events filled the next few weeks, during which I met more of Grey's relatives, visited the rest of the family's estates, and even made a trip without Grey to spend a weekend with Jeriah, Seena, and the kids.

I had a wonderful, whirlwind time that first holiday as a citizen. I was happy to be alive. I loved being loved. With no obligation to the military, I had no commitments, no job to return to. I was free to simply enjoy myself.

And then it was over.

The delightful newness of my retirement had worn off. I'd learned what I needed to know about living as a CFC wife and had established myself in a comfortable routine. My boredom became desperate.

I considered going to see Jeriah. Like me, he'd left the service after ten years. He took a civilian security job in Centre City.

Unfortunately, with all the people who'd poured in from Arkentak and the surrounding regions, housing was hard to come by. Seena and the kids were still in Saltcreek Point, while Jeriah shared a flat with two other men. Visiting him was out of the question until he found a place of his own.

I invited him to come see us, but he declined. He said every time he could get away, he went to see his family. I couldn't argue with that.

I missed working. I missed Jeriah. I missed Naka.

And much of the time, I missed Grey, because now that we were settled, he was gone a lot. All day, almost every day, often until late at night, and not infrequently, all night. He could no longer discuss his work with me, and I didn't ask.

And so I drank.

❧ Chapter 13 ❧

PULLED FROM THE BURROW-RAT HOLE

HEARD A NOISE, dimly, as if a thick blanket were over my head. What was that?

I opened my eyes, and my head pounded. The only light came from the aquarium above me as I sprawled across the settee. That, and the glittering city lights outside the window. But I heard footsteps in the dark.

I tried to sit, but the anvil on my head pressed me down. Did that moan come from me? I had to shake this. Someone was in my house.

I forced myself to sit. "Who's there?" My stomach churned, and my voice sounded like it came from the grave. A light came on in the kitchen. Cabinet doors opened and closed.

I wanted to stand but couldn't figure out how. The settee seemed to hold me in its grasp.

Heavy footsteps approached. My stomach heaved. I tried to move, but the only thing to come up was my stomach contents—which splashed into a bucket that miraculously appeared in front of me.

The next thing I remember was waking up in bed, in my nightclothes. The smell of sizzling sausage made my stomach curdle.

I rose slowly and shuffled to the living room, avoiding the kitchen. Grey was in there. Food was in there. I didn't need either one right now.

I went to the aquarium and looked for a slugfin. There used to be a bunch of them in there, creeping along the bottom of the tank. Why couldn't I find one? The movement of the fish made me dizzy, but I kept searching, holding myself up by the back of the settee.

Grey's heavy tread announced his presence, but he didn't say anything at first. After a moment, he asked, "What are you doing?"

"Looking for a slugfin. I can't find one."

"There should be a dozen of them. I bought them to help keep the tank clean."

"Yeah, they're good for that. Why don't I see any?"

He joined me in the search. "I don't either. But what difference does it make? Come into the dining room. I've made breakfast."

My eyes filled with tears. "You're so good to me. I should be makin' you breakfush."

His jaw tightened. "You're still drunk."

"A little. Maybe. That's why I want a slugfin."

"That makes no sense. What do you want one for?"

"To eat it. If you swallow it whole, it absorbs the alcohol and sobers you up quicker. Makes your breath smell better too."

He nodded. "Ah. That explains it."

"'Splains what?"

"Why sometimes when I come home, you smell like a fish drowned in alcohol. And why there aren't any slugfins left. You've probably already swallowed them all."

I couldn't look at him. That wasn't true, was it? Had I eaten all of them? And if I had, could he really have smelled the booze on me? "There have to be some left. They're just hiding." I put my hand on the tank. "Here, fishy fishy…"

He took me by the shoulders and turned me away. "Come into the dining room. A strong cup of crim works just as well, and real food is even better."

Confused, I let him walk me out of the sitting room like a shuffling robot. "You cooked breakfast?"

"Sausage and eggs. And crim." He pulled out a chair. "Sit."

I sat. "I don't get drunk, you know. I don't know why it happened this time."

He put a sausage on a plate and cut it into small pieces. "I imagine it has something to do with the empty bottle of whisky I found in the recycle bin and the half-empty one in the cabinet."

"Oh. That's good stuff. But I thought I'd just opened it. Is it really half empty?"

He put a spoonful of scrambled eggs on the plate, then set it in front of me. "It had better be good, for the hundred and sixty urexi you paid for it."

I stared at the food. It seemed to swim on the plate. I rubbed my eyes. "How do you know how much it cost?"

"I keep an eye on my expenditures." He set a cup of crim in front of me. "This is cooled enough that it won't scald you. I know how you hate to burn your mouth."

I took a sip. "Mm. You're so good to me."

"I don't know. Am I?" He moved a chair near me and sat very close.

"Yes, you're good to me. You make me breakfast. Give me glaffcrim."

He pointed to my plate. "Eat."

I didn't think I was hungry, but once I started, I couldn't eat fast enough. When I picked up my plate to lick off the grease, Grey took it from me gently. "I'm glad you liked it."

I looked into my empty cup. "Is there more crim?"

"You may have all the glaffcrim you like." He took my plate and utensils into the kitchen, returned with the crim pot, and refilled both our cups. Then he sat beside me again. "Let's talk."

I put my head down on my arms. "I'm not feeling so good."

"Small wonder. But we're going to talk."

"I think I ate too fast."

"You did. Are you going to be sick?"

I shook my head, which amounted to wobbling it on my arms. "Didn't you say there's still some of that good whisky left?"

"That's what we have to talk about."

I lifted my head. "What?"

He took in a breath as if to brace himself. "I told you I would be with you if your brain worms wake up. Remember?"

I suddenly felt very sober. "Not if. When. They always wake up."

He arched his brows, prodding me to answer his question.

"Yes, I remember. Why?"

"I'm willing to go through that with you, no matter how bitter the end may be. But I'm not willing to watch you drink yourself to death."

I frowned. "What are you talking about?"

"You know perfectly well what I'm talking about. I've warned you about your drinking before, more than once. And you know how I dislike repeating myself."

I put my head back down. Yes, I knew that, but he was going to repeat himself anyway.

"Your drinking has always concerned me. But now, it's out of control."

I spoke into my arms. "It's not that bad."

"When I came home yesterday, you were passed out on the settee and you smelled like a distillery. I call that out of control."

I lifted my head. My stomach roiled. "That's not fair. How can you say that?" I'd have stormed out of the room, but my legs felt like rubber.

"Don't be angry." He took my hands and kissed them. "The fault is mine. If I were a better husband, I wouldn't drive you to drink. What do you need? What can I do for you?"

I'd have thought he was mocking me, but his expression was sincere.

"Drive me to drink? You don't drive me to anything. You—you're perfect." I pulled my hands from between his wonderful, strong warm ones and ran my fingers along his noble face, tracing his neatly trimmed beard with my thumbs.

He took my hands in his again. "No. I'm a long way from perfect." His shake of the head was almost imperceptible. "You need something, and I don't know what it is. Help me." His deep, dark eyes pleaded. "Help me to help you."

My mouth hung open in a stare until my tongue dried out. Or maybe it felt dry because of the whisky. But my mind was a complete blank. I could think of nothing to say. Nothing at all. I went from staring to crying, and he gathered me into his arms and I sobbed into his shirt until it was soaked, and I couldn't figure what was happening.

I tried to say, "I never get drunk," and "I never cry," but I couldn't get out the words because I was too drunk and crying too hard, and the impossibility of it all made me sob all the more.

⁂

I WAS TOO much of a mess for our conversation to go very far that morning. But in the evening, while sitting together in the media room, he shut off the video screen at the end of the grappleball game to resume our talk.

It did not start off to my liking.

While I'd been in my stupor, Grey had dumped out all the alcohol in the house. Even the good stuff that cost a hundred sixty a bottle. Even the wine I'd thought was well hidden.

Upon learning this, my first thought was a highly indignant, *What a terrible waste!* An instant later, I thought, *No problem. I can replace it.* Money wasn't an issue, and the Beverage Bureau offered delivery. I pretended to be upset, but I wasn't as furious as I would have been if I hadn't had that option.

Until he told me I was banned at the Bureau. Translation: no store in the world could provide me with a bottle, nor bar in the land could serve me, without risk of being shut down by the City ban enforcers. Grey could buy a drink for me in a restaurant, but I couldn't buy it myself.

A Bureau ban expires after a year. I tried to imagine going a year with only an occasional drink. Yes, I could do it. I went without either alcohol or crim the whole time I was in Land Forces foundational training, and I didn't have much opportunity to drink when on active duty. So I knew I *could* go without it, but I didn't want to. Didn't think I should have to. It angered me that he would go to such lengths.

And I let him know it with a fury that was hot and genuine.

His face reddened, but otherwise, he maintained complete control. "This will be a civil discussion. If you can't do that, you may go to bed, and we'll try again in the morning."

"You're sending me to my room?" I'm pretty sure I screamed the words. "Like a child?"

"No, I am asking that we sit and talk like adults. If you prefer to throw a tantrum, you may do it elsewhere. I do not wish to see it."

I was almost shaking with anger. A tantrum would have been easy, but I had just enough sense to see that if I acted like a child, I couldn't object to being treated like a one.

Beneath his dark, unsparing gaze, I took a couple of deep breaths. "Okay. We can talk. But what am I supposed to say? A Bureau ban? That's— that's— it's humiliating." My eyes burned with tears.

"And passing out stone-drunk isn't?"

I turned my face away and clenched my teeth. I wouldn't let his exaggeration get to me.

"Or swallowing crap-eating fish to try to cover it up? Swallowing them live?"

"It works. You never knew what I was doing until—"

His tone sharpened enough to cut. "You want to be a drunk like your father? Like your brother Ibro? People say all Freemans are drunks. By marrying you, I stood up and said that's not true." He paced, gesturing. "And when I come home and smell alcohol on you, night after night, it hurts me like — like a lash tearing a strip of skin from my back. You're killing yourself, Jemima. And it's killing me. You think you have the right to do that, to kill us both?"

He stood looking down on me, his face twisted in agony.

I'd heard little after *a drunk like your father...like Ibro...* But at his impassioned pause, I listened to a mental play-back of the rest.

And by some miracle, I heard it.

Looking into his eyes, I saw him writhing in pain.

Pain that I caused.

Jeriah was worried Grey would hurt *me*? We were a mismatch for sure, but Riah had it backwards.

"It is humiliating." My voice was hoarse with tears. "But not for me. It's humiliating for you. That you lied to them."

He sat beside me on the sofa. "Lied to them? Lied to whom? What do you mean, lied?"

"Lied to your family. To the world. They were right. All Freemans *are* drunks. Marrying me doesn't change that. It just makes you look like a fool for doing it."

He tried to take me into his arms, but I pushed him away. "Which is funny, because you're not a fool." I stood up to distance myself from him. "You're a good man, Ashgrey Standtall. But you have terrible taste in women." I tugged at my wedding bracelet. It would have been a nice dramatic flourish if I could have slipped it off and thrown it at him, but it was designed to stay where it was. "You might as well try changing a dragon into a daisy. It ain't gonna happen. Give up on me." I turned toward the bedroom with every intention of packing a bag. "I'm going back to Freemansland where I belong."

For a big man, he was surprisingly fast. I'd hardly taken a step before he'd grabbed my wrist—the one with the bracelet I'd tried to slip off—and spun me around. "You're not going anywhere."

He pulled me against him, nose to nose. "Why are you afraid of being loved?"

I was too surprised at the question to have a ready answer. Before I could think of one, my face was in his hands and his mouth covered mine, and I couldn't have gotten a word out if I'd had one.

Grey had some, though. In small spurts, he released the pressure enough to say, "I will never... give up... on you."

That evening, I learned the media room can be used for something other than video entertainment, and Grey learned that a floor can be used as a bed.

Despite the plush carpet, however, the floor was hard under my still-achy pelvis. So afterward, I rolled on top of Grey and sprawled like a cat on a cushion.

He ran his fingertips up and down my back in a light, lazy way. The contented sound that rumbled from me wasn't exactly a purr, but it got the point across.

"So we're good?" His voice was as soft as his touch.

"We're very good." I thought a moment then said, "No, *you're* very good. And if you're fool enough to want me around, I'm happy to humor you."

"Hey, none of that." He rolled me over onto my back, then sat up. "Look around you." His wave encompassed the room. "Do I bring anything into my home that's not quality?"

I sat too. "This floor's hard. Despite its obvious quality."

I started to clamber to my feet but Grey stood first and helped me up. "How about the couch?"

He pulled me down onto it, and we lay together, with Grey's feet hanging off the end.

I snuggled against him. "I thought we were getting up."

His fingers caressed my skin, his words my ear. "What's your hurry?"

"No hurry."

"Good. Because we have to talk some more."

"Oh. That went so well the last time."

"It ended well, though, don't you think?"

"Yes, but—" I struggled to rise. "I've got to get up and move around. My hips ache like a tooth."

We got up and dressed, then walked a few laps around the little park across from the building. Though a warm night for early spring, I found it chilly and was glad of the winter coat I'd put on. Between the street lamps surrounding the park and the illuminated fountain in the center, it was sufficiently lit for a nighttime stroll.

We walked in silence until I asked, "So what did you want to argue about next?"

"Nothing. I never want to argue with you." He pulled me against him in a one-armed hug. "Even though I do enjoy the eventual resolution."

"So what did you want to *not* argue about?"

"I want to know what I can do for you. How I can make you happy, so you don't look to a bottle to supply whatever I'm lacking."

Our steps matched perfectly. I laid my head on his shoulder. "You do make me happy. Every moment you're with me."

"How about when I'm gone? Am I away too much?"

I paused. "Yes and no. Yes, because I miss you when you're gone. But no, because I lived in that world too, not long ago. I understand why you're gone, and why you can't talk about it."

"Yes, that was your world too. And now it's not. And you're bored, aren't you?"

"Oh, I don't know…"

"Why won't you say it? You don't know what to do with yourself."

"But I shouldn't be like that. I have everything I need. How could I want anything else?

"We all need a purpose."

I had to think about that for a minute or two. "You know what I planned to do when I first joined the Land Forces?"

"Serve ten years and become a Citizen of Merit."

"Yes. And once I'd accomplished that? You know what my grand ambition was?"

"I don't believe you've ever told me. What was this glorious dream?"

"All I ever wanted, all I ever thought about from the time the City took me under their wing, was to go back to Freedom and live on the stillwater like I used to."

He said nothing at first, and neither did I. Then he said softly, "I'm sorry I spoiled your plans."

"It wasn't a plan. It was a non-plan. It was an instinctive animal response. Like when you pull a burrowrat out of its hole, and all it wants to do is go back into it. Even when you put a big fat spineworm in front of it—that's its favorite food, you know—even if you lay a spineworm on its nose, it only wants to get back down in its hole. You know what I did once?" I lapsed into the Freemansland dialect, as it seemed appropriate for my story. "One night, when it was dark, I dug up a whole bunch of spineys, about a dozen of 'em, and laid 'em all on a big flat rock so they couldn't dig back down into the ground. Then I stuck my hand in a burrowrat's hole, grabbed that ol' rat by its head, and drug him out."

"Didn't it bite you?"

"Sure, but what did I care? I wanted to see if he'd stop and eat the feast I'd fixed for 'im. And y'know what? I put that rat up there on the rock with all them spineys, and he knocked half of 'em off the rock and out of his way, he was in such a hurry to get back home."

I resumed speaking in my usual, more Citified manner. "I was that burrowrat. I didn't care that life was better outside of my hole. I wanted the familiar, dirty walls around me. I kept thinking I'd be safe there, if only I could get back."

"And now?"

I had to consider how to answer, because I wasn't sure. "Now, I feel safest when I'm with you. Even when you're not with me, though, I know you're with me. Like—like after the bomb, and I was in another sort of hole, I saw you there, because you were with me in my heart, in my mind, and it made me feel better. Does that make any sense?"

He nodded slowly. "I think. But I don't understand how you could have felt safe before. You tell me about this little girl, outdoors at night alone, digging in the dirt, doing her own sort of research on rodent behavior, as if you're talking about a child in a nice clean schoolroom watching a caged jerblin run on a wheel. How old were you then?"

"Probably about six or seven."

"I'd love to go back in time and change all that. I wish I could swoop down and take you and your brother both from your grandma when she was climbing that long stairway up the sharpfall—is that what you call it? A sharpfall?"

I nodded.

"I wish I could have taken you two precious little babies and given you to a family who would nurture and care for you as children should be cared for. So then, when I met you later, you wouldn't want to run and hide in a bottle. So you wouldn't be afraid of real freedom."

I'd listened in growing agitation until I could no longer keep quiet. "Real freedom? Oh, don't get me started on that. You don't know what freedom is if you think it starts with yanking babies from their grandmother's arms." I lowered my voice, knowing what I was about to say shouldn't be overheard. "The City thinks they can force freedom on people. It might be your definition of freedom, but it feels like something else to the country you're blasting into the ground."

Grey's reply was low as well, but colder than the air. "I am going to forget you said that."

"No, don't forget it. Don't ever forget it."

We walked in tense silence for several minutes, until Grey took my hand in his—gently. "What is freedom, then? If not the opportunity to better yourself?"

"I have no idea. But I know what it isn't."

After another thoughtful silence, he said, "Let's leave it undefined, for now. Until we come up with a meaning we can agree on, I have a suggestion."

"Concerning what?"

"You're not a burrowrat, nor any other kind of beast. You have a very human need—to pursue a goal."

I nodded. "We agree on that, at least."

"Being a woman of privilege limits you. You needn't struggle to earn a living, and you have people to do all your mundane work. If you had a huge estate to manage, as Mimma does, or a business to help your husband with, like your Aunt Lanie, it wouldn't be a problem. But as it is now, your day-to-day activities aren't enough."

"Please don't say I should buy a business, because I hate business. I don't know how Aunt Lanie stands it. Unless it's a fishing business. I might be able to get into that—"

He chuckled. "You'd eat all the profits. No, I'm thinking more along the lines of what Papa was talking about."

"I've heard him talk about a lot of things. What, specific—" As I mentally scrolled through our most recent conversation, it hit me. "Oh, you mean about writing children's stories? That's crazy."

"Why? You're a good writer, you've got more stories than a bird has songs, and you might not enjoy children, but you can tell a tale in way that holds their attention."

I was ready to get out of the cold, so I led the way through the park and across the road to our building. "All I know how to write is term papers and reports and things. I wouldn't have the first idea how to go about writing books for children."

"The Creative Arts College should be taking registration for the summer term about now. You might check into it. See what their creative writing program involves." The doorman nodded to us and opened the door, and Grey handed him a tip card to scan.

Once we were inside, I said quietly, "I usually forget to do that. It seems so strange to tip someone just to open the door."

"I know. He's told me. When you forget, I tip him double."

"Sounds pretty lucrative. Maybe I'll just take a job as a doorman."

We waited for the elevator. "You can't. You're a citizen."

"So I can only spend money, not earn it."

"That's right. Our urexi support the whole world."

The part of it we're not blowing up. I kept that subversive thought to myself because the elevator operator—who Grey also tipped when we exited—would have overheard me. Considering the current climate, part of his job might be to keep his eyes and ears open for anything suspicious.

Grey opened our apartment door. "There's another reason I think you should take some writing classes."

"What's that?"

"It will give you a chance to make some friends. You don't know anyone around here yet, and it's not healthy to be alone all the time."

The thought cheered me. A friend might be persuaded to buy me a drink now and then.

I didn't want to act too excited, though, so I just grunted. "Apparently I'm naturally drawn to an unhealthy lifestyle."

"Apparently."

I'd hoped he'd contradict me and was a little put out that he didn't. But he made no further comment as he pulled up the Creative Arts College on his tablet.

I sat beside him and looked at the screen. "That school's for Citizens only, right?"

He nodded as he scrolled.

"So you want me to make friends, but not from the lower classes."

"I want you to be happy. I want you to love your life." He turned his attention from the screen to me. "The one you're living now, not the one you keep trying to run back to." His dark eyes sought my gaze, and found it. "I want you to love being loved by me."

❧ Chapter 14 ❧

—∽∽—

THINGS GET TENSE

—∽∽—

AND NOW WE JUMP AHEAD five years.

You surely have the next part figured out anyway. After all, my eight-book Stillwater series was the biggest thing to ever hit the world of young people's literature. Even if you haven't read any of the books, you've probably seen a film, played a video game, or at least heard references to the Stillwater stories.

Nevertheless, in case you've been living in a burrowrat hole for the past couple of decades, I'll provide a brief overview.

Written under the pen name J. S. Freeman (the "S" being for Standtall), the first four books are for younger children, beginning on the fourth-rank level and progressing through the sixth. The last four are for older kids. My thought was for readers to grow up with the characters, a twin boy and girl living on Freedom a generation before the City took it over. When Freedom was free.

In the publishing world, Stillwater was groundbreaking in a number of respects: it was the first progressive-reader series; the first of any fictional work set in Freemansland; the first with Freemanslanders as the good guys rather than buffoons or villains;

and the first released by a Centre City publishing house that did not glorify the City.

The amazing thing was, Brick House Publishing wasn't owned by the Standtall family. I was an unknown to them, and they took a gamble on me.

And they won.

So, five years after enrolling in a creative writing course out of desperate boredom and to humor my husband, I was on my way to being one of the most well-known writers in the world.

I only drank socially. I had a reason to get up in the morning, work I was excited about, and a husband I adored as much as he adored me.

I think I might have been happy.

ADDRESSING A COUPLE hundred school children in the fourth through sixth ranks was never something I looked forward to.

But this group was different from most I faced: among the sixth-rankers, my niece Kyee Jem beamed up at me with glowing pride. At eleven years old, she was becoming a beautiful girl. I had a hard time looking out at the whole audience instead of speaking only to her.

Wrapping up my short talk, I lifted a book high. "Remember in the stories, how books on Freemansland aren't made out of regular paper? Well, Brick House Publishing has just issued a special edition of the first title in the Stillwater series. The books are made of the same waterproof *banroo* skin as the ones Tia and Tuu in the stories read, and they're bound with the same waterproof materials." I opened the book and turned a few pages to demonstrate. "We're donating this copy of *The Papevine Twins* to your school's library, so you can all have a chance to see and handle it."

Some of the kids strained to get a better look. I thought a few of the older ones pretended to look bored, but failed.

I set the book down. "Mrs. Oakwood says we have a little time left, so if anyone has any questions—"

Dozens of kids clamored, their arms raised high.

"Tell you what. Let's hear from one girl and one boy from each rank. Since I'm a girl, I'll start with a girl. A girl from the fourth rank. Who has a question?"

The questions were similar every time I spoke to a school group, so I had ready answers. *Are you the real Tia in the story?* No, I made her up. She's a pretend person.

Do you really have a twin brother? Yes, I do, but I'm not Tia, and he's not Tuu.

Have you ever seen a dragon? Yes, many times.

Did your father really hunt them? I'm not Tia, and the Papa in the story isn't my father.

And then there was the favorite: *Is it true they didn't wear clothes?* I explained that it was hot and wet on Freemansland. People didn't need clothes to keep warm, wet clothes are uncomfortable, and the way things get moldy and rotten in those conditions, you wouldn't be able to wear a shirt very many times before it fell apart. "So," I'd say, "it was easier to just forget about clothing." The kids' reaction to that always amused me.

I got some new questions this time, mostly about the fact that KJ was my niece. But one prim and proper sixth-rank girl asked with disapproval, "How many animals do you have to kill to make one of those books?"

It took me a second to realize what she was talking about. "Oh, you mean the waterproof books with the banroo skin pages? It's called skin, but it's not from an animal. Banroo is a plant, and it's plentiful all over Freemansland. They cut it down, chop it up, and boil it in big pots. Then they pour it out into great big flat trays. As the liquid cools, a tough fibrous layer forms on top. That's called a skin. They pull off the skin, stretch it and dry it, and that's what they use for paper on Freemansland. They have regular paper now, too, but they still use banroo skin for some things."

I smiled at the girl, who didn't look like she believed me. "So don't worry. No animals died to make this book."

Someone else asked, "Why don't they just use real paper?"

"Because it's so wet all the time. If you leave an ordinary book out in the rain, it gets ruined. But Tia and Tuu can carry their books in a pouring rain or drop them in the water and they won't be damaged."

A boy called out without raising his hand. "What's the matter with electronic books?"

A teacher spoke to him sharply. "Wait to be recognized."

But I'd already started answering. "Water ruins electronics even more than it does paper. But besides that, Tia and Tuu live in a time when there were no electronics on Freemansland. No computers, no televisions, no video games."

The children went wide-eyed. I heard assorted murmurs ranging from *Huuuh?* and *That's awful!* to *Wouldn't they die?* and *How did they watch the Ellerja Games?*

Before I'd sorted out their questions, the principal, Mrs. Oakwood, came forward to call the assembly to a close. "That's all we have time for, children. You've been very attentive, and I'm proud of you. Let's show Ms. Freeman how much we appreciate her visit with a round of applause."

And so ended my second school appearance of the day. From there, I had another talk at a public library, and I didn't get back to Riah's house until evening.

Riah never found a place for his family to live in Centre City, as he'd planned when taking his new job. After six months, his employer allowed him to transfer to their office in Saltcreek Point.

He and Sheena now lived near where they'd lived before, but in a larger house.

After the autocab dropped me off, I climbed the front steps and rang the bell. I'd thought this a nice neighborhood the first time I visited, but the CFC life had changed my perspective. Now everything seemed small and shabby.

Seena called, "Come on in, it's open," but she came to the door anyway. "Jeriah's not here. He's working late tonight." She let me in, then bolted the door. "Did you eat? Can I get you anything?"

"No, I grabbed a bite, thanks. Just need to sit and unwind. It's been a long day." Nothing stressed me out like being around a bunch of kids.

Jeo jumped up and down in front of me. "Play with me, Auntie Jem. I wanna play Beastie Bash."

"Hu-uh." KJ shoved him away. "We're playin' Cross the Bridge, 'cause Auntie Jem likes that game better."

"I wanna play Beastie Bash! Auntie Jem, play Beastie with me!"

Seena grabbed them each by the ear and twisted. "Nobody's playing anything if you don't settle down right now."

They did, wincing, and I said quickly, "I see no reason why we can't play one game of each. Mama? Will you play with us?"

Seena let them go and they stood rubbing their ears and frowning. Jeo's lip jutted out, but he held back the tears.

"If they can behave themselves, they can play one game of each. But I can't. I've got a kitchen to clean up and laundry to do."

When the kids ran off to grab their games, I told Seena, "Leave it for now. I can help you after they go to bed."

She shook her head. "No, if you keep them happy for me, that's all the help I need."

I admit it. I'm a terrible auntie. I'd rather clean the kitchen and do laundry than play with children, especially after having spent the day enduring wave after wave of squirming juveniles. But I was overruled.

Two games later, they more or less obediently went off to bed. I got the impression ear-twisting wasn't the worst thing they'd experienced at their mother's hand, and they didn't seem inclined to test her patience that night. Good thing, too, because I didn't care to see what might happen if they did.

Once they were quiet in their rooms, Seena got out a bottle of wine and two glasses. "Still need to unwind?"

"More than ever, thanks." I mentally slapped myself. "I mean, they're great kids. I'm just not used to them. I don't know how to deal with all that energy."

We went into the sitting room. Decorated with simple good taste, the room was no bigger than my clothes closet, and the furniture was low-end, but Seena was a meticulous housekeeper. She opened the wine and picked up a glass. "Am I allowed to give you this?"

"Legally, you mean? Of course. The ban only applies to business establishments." To my chagrin, Grey had renewed the Bureau Ban every year since he started it. But I didn't like to talk about that. "Your house always looks so nice. I don't know how you do it, on your feet all day at the bakery, then coming home and doing housework and everything."

She stared at me as she handed me the glass as if trying to decide how to answer. "Thanks," she finally said.

Well, that was weird. Maybe try something else. "KJ and Jeo are loveable kids. I'll bet they keep you from getting lonely when Riah's gone, don't they?"

"Something like that."

I sipped the cheap wine without pleasure. Somewhere a clock ticked. A car drove past the house. Seena drank too. She didn't look at me.

"I'm sorry, is there something wrong?"

She shook her head. "Not that I can see."

I set down my glass. No coaster necessary, as the tabletop wasn't real wood. "Seena. I thought we were friends. We used to be, anyway. You can talk to me."

She looked at me then. "What do you want me to say? Sitting there in your perfect make-up and your three-hundred-urexi shoes. That same skinny butt in its bespoke dress perched on my tacky old sofa also sits at a fancy dinner table in Centre City with Council Ministers. And you ask me what's wrong?"

I didn't tell her I'd paid more than twice three hundred for my shoes, nor that I wouldn't be seen in CFC company in this two-year-old dress. Erroneous assumptions aside, I couldn't fathom where such vehemence came from. "What's any of that got to do with anything? We were roommates. We're family. Who cares what I wear or how much I pay for shoes? I don't look down on you. I'm here, aren't I? Or don't you want me here? I don't understand."

She drained her glass. "I'm fat and dumpy, aren't I?"

"No," I lied. "You don't look sixteen anymore, but neither do I. You know, don't you, that it was you who taught me how to wear make-up. And to fix my hair. You taught me how to *not* look dumpy."

She poured herself another. "You and your brother. You're both so good-looking. I don't know why he married me."

"Because he fell off a cliff in love with you. He's still crazy about you, Seena. When we're on the phone, it's you and the kids he talks about."

"Really?" A hopeful expression seemed to ask permission to come out, but she didn't grant it. "He's gone so much, though. Sometimes I wonder..."

"It's his job, hon. Grey's gone a lot too. They can't talk about their work, but they're both good at it, and what they do is important. Even if it means they're not home much."

My empathy seemed to cheer Seena a little, so I went on. "We're both in the same boat. It's lonely at night, though, isn't it?"

"Same boat? We might be in the same water, but our boats dock in different ports." She stood. "Can I get you anything else before I go to bed?"

I stood too. "Yes. I'd like the chance to help you. Why don't you and the kids come stay with me for awhile? It would be good for all of us to spend more time together."

She narrowed her eyes and spoke low. "I don't need your sliming charity."

When she tried to step around me, I blocked her path. "I'm not offering you any *sliming charity*. You're my oldest friend. You're my brother's wife. I want to be a sister to you."

"No, thanks. I've got a sister, and she lives on Freemansland. When she invites me to visit, I know she means it. She's not just taking pity on me."

There was plenty I could have said to that, but I'd be sorry if I did. So all I said was, "Thanks for the wine. I'll get my things and call a cab."

I COMPLETED MY book tour a couple of days later, then had a meeting with my editor, Krad Alskar, and illustrator, Jena Trebb, at Brick House Publishing.

Krad was wonderful. He knew what it took to make my writing sing. But I credit Jena's marvelous illustrations for my initial success. I couldn't believe the way she captured exactly what was in my head and put it on the page in such a delightful way. Each succeeding book had fewer illustrations, of course, until books five through eight had none at all. But she did the covers on all of them, and I couldn't have been happier with the result.

This meeting was to discuss the artwork for *Sunset on the Stillwater*, the fourth title, as well as the format and cover style for the second half of the series. I was well under way with book six at that point and had a good idea of where I wanted to go with the rest.

We had a productive meeting, but I was glad when it was over, as I was eager to get home. By this time, Grey had left the service after putting in twenty years. Now he worked for the investigative branch of Ministry Security.

He was out of town, but he expected to get back about the same time I did. When I envisioned our reunion, I smiled inside and out.

He was on a quiet assignment—that is, out of contact—so I wasn't sure which of us would get there first, but I didn't care. I just looked forward to seeing him.

No, that's not quite true. In one respect, I hoped he'd get there first, because it took him a while to decompress after he came home. Maybe I'd come in and find him already relaxed and happy.

On the other hand, he might not like coming home to an empty house. That might make his mood darken even more.

It wasn't like that when he was in the IA, but since working for Ministry Security, he was always strung tight. Clearly, his new job was stressful, so I did everything I could to massage the kinks out of his temper. Sometimes, though, the best thing to do was keep my distance until his ill humor ran its course. On those occasions, he spent a lot of time in his weight room and wore out a pair of gloves on his punching bag. Sometimes I wondered whose faces he pretended he pounded.

In the autocab on my way home, my phone rang. I grabbed it, saw it was Grey, and answered eagerly. "Hey, hon, you home?"

His, "What?" was somewhere between a bark and a growl. "You're not?"

"I'm in a cab. Just left a meeting at Brick House. I'll be home in forty-five minutes. Where are you?"

"Oh, yeah." His tone softened. "I forgot. How was your book tour?"

"It went well. It'll be good to be home, though. I miss you."

"I miss you too. I called to tell you there's been a delay. I'll be home tonight, but it won't be until late."

I wilted into the seat. I should be glad he was all right, that he was coming home. But I didn't like that word *delay*. "Thanks for letting me know. I'll wait up for you."

"No need. I won't be good for anything until I've had some sleep. But unless something unexpected comes up, I should be home for at least a week."

"Oh, that's good—"

"Sorry, gotta go. Don't wait up."

He disconnected, leaving me holding my glowing phone. Disappointed, I slipped it into my bag. He was safe. He'd be home. And despite what he said, I'd be up to greet him when he got there.

I had the car stop at the market and wait while I bought the ingredients for Grey's favorite pasta and beef dish. I wanted to have it waiting for him in case he was hungry.

When I got home, I unpacked my bags, then cooked. For my own supper, I ate pasta and sauce without the beef. Finally, with the kitchen clean and everything in order as Grey liked it, I set up camp on the settee with a tall glass of pink nimrelade—my favorite nonalcoholic beverage—and the latest release by Sejam Rench, one of my favorite authors. It might be several hours before Grey got home, but I'd make the best of the wait.

Last time I looked at the clock, it was 23:30. Some time after that, my eyes grew too heavy to keep open, so I closed them, just for a minute.

I dreamed the door opened and Grey came in. When I heard him standing above me, saying, "What the... what the slime!" I realized it wasn't a dream.

I opened my eyes. The clock said 2:12, and the dark shadow of his bulky form strode away with grim purpose. I sat up. "Grey?"

He didn't answer, but I heard him enter the kitchen, where the light came on. A cabinet door opened. "What's this?"

Suddenly wide awake, I grabbed my empty glass and followed him. "I meant to wait up for you, but I fell asleep."

He held a half-empty brandy bottle, his face stormy and his voice like thunder. "Where did this come from?"

"It was a gift from your brother, remember? He and Pearl brought it when they visited a couple months ago. We opened it when they were here, and no one's touched it since."

His accusing gaze took in the glass in my hands then shifted to my face.

Flushing hot, I thrust the glass toward him. "Nimrelade. Want to smell it?"

He stared at me, but his frown seemed to be more from confusion than anger.

I went to him, set the glass on the counter, and tipped my face up to his. "You won't smell alcohol on me. Nor dead fish, either."

His frown melted into a weary slack-face, and he relaxed his death grip on the bottle.

I took it before he dropped it, set it beside my glass, then put my arms around him. "Rough trip, huh?"

He pulled me close and buried his face in my neck. "I'm sorry. I shouldn't have accused you."

"It's okay, I know what it must have looked like."

"I jumped to conclusions." He didn't relax his hug. If anything, he held me tighter.

"You're tired. And besides, you said not to wait up for you, but I did anyway. Tried to, at least."

"I should have trusted you." He still spoke into my neck.

"And if you keep holding me like that, you're going to suffocate me."

He loosened his hold but didn't let go. "That better?"

"Yes." His heart pounded hard and fast against my ear. "You okay?"

He nodded. "Now I am. I'm sorry."

The thrumming in his chest slowed, but it was still rapid. His heart must have been ready to burst a minute ago.

I lifted my face and kissed him. "Let's go t—"

He smothered the rest of the sentence with more kisses than I could handle.

❧ Chapter 15 ❧

THE DEATH CHAIR

T HE NEXT AFTERNOON, Grey and I went over our accounts in preparation for an appointment with our financial advisor the following morning.

While we worked in the office, the doorman buzzed. "I'm sorry, Mr. and Mrs. Standtall, but some gentlemen are on their way up. I couldn't stop them."

Grey's heavy brows rose. "What gentlemen?"

"From Ministry Security. Two are coming your way, and two are standing here with me, sir, allowing me to make this call. I expect your visitors will be there about now."

"Thank you." The door chime rang as Gray disconnected, and he rose. "Stay here," he told me on his way to the foyer.

I remained in the office but strained to listen to what was going on. The door opened, and an unfamiliar man's voice said, "Ashgrey Standtall?"

It sounded like the men didn't wait for an invitation but barged right in. "We need you and your wife to come with us, sir."

My heart leapt, and Grey's barked order to stay put lost its bite. I hurried through the house into the foyer. "What's going on?"

"Mrs. Standtall?" There were four men, not two as the doorman had said. Their expressions were grim as a death sentence. "We need to see your identification."

Grey had his out already, and one of the men took it from him. My mind reeled. "I'll go get it." When I turned toward the bedroom to get my purse, one of the men went with me.

This was wrong. How could they invade our house like this? Demanding to see ID in our own home? But Grey worked for the same agency, and he didn't dispute their authority. So, as much as my mind rebelled, I complied.

I snatched my purse from the dresser, pulled out the folder, and handed it to the goon who had followed me into the bedroom. "Here."

He took it, gave it a good once-over, scanned it with some small device, then pocketed it. "It's in order, ma'am. But I must ask you to come with us."

I felt dizzy. "I don't understand."

"Please, ma'am. We need you to come immediately."

Why wasn't Grey arguing? I stormed past the man back to the foyer. "Grey, what are they doing? What's going on?"

His face pale, he grabbed me and pulled me close. "We have to go."

With two men in front and two behind, we hustled along the hall to the emergency stairway, then down and out through the rear door of the building, where a limo waited along with two other cars. As soon as Grey and I were in the back of the limo, all three cars took off.

A white-bearded man sat in the shadows. I recognized him as Elip Hold, one of the three heads of the Council of Fathers.

When Grey saw him, he sat up straighter. "Father Hold, sir! I am sorry, I was not aware you were here."

The Father sounded shaky. "I am sorry, Ashgrey. It is my sad duty to inform you that your father—" His voice broke. "Minister Standtall was gunned down by an assassin a short time ago. We are bringing your family in for protection, as well as the other ministers and their families, until we can be sure no one else is in danger."

⁂

I WON'T TELL you the location of the compound. Only that it seemed very secure. That is to say, I felt like a prisoner.

How could I not, after being whisked from my home with nothing but my purse in hand and the clothes on my back? Carried away in a car with blacked-out windows? Given almost no information as to what was happening? If I'd tried to escape, I couldn't have gotten far without my ID, which the men refused to give back. For all practical purposes, we were captives of Ministry Security.

Mimma was at the compound when we arrived, with Grey's sister Silver, her husband Fenn, and their children. Bark and Pearl arrived a short time later with their brood.

We all sat with Mimma without speaking much. We couldn't fathom what we'd heard. Stal Standtall, Minister of Domestic Peace, assassinated? I kept expecting him to come in and reassure us it was all a mistake, and I think the others felt the same way.

Other ministers and their families were brought to the compound, with the last of them arriving late that night. All told, the facility housed seventy-two adults and thirty-nine children as "honored guests," plus servants hired by Ministry Security to take care of us. We were told another facility housed the remainder of the official families, around two hundred fifty in all. Janren Stock, Minister Standtall's former Underminister and now the new Minister of Domestic Peace, was among the other group.

Considering it was constructed for the highest ranked people in the world, the place was surprisingly plain. The gray painted walls held no artwork, and industrial carpeting covered the concrete floors. The sturdy design of the furnishings and household goods seemed more for function than aesthetics. The bedding and towels, at least, were soft, and the toiletries, if not top shelf, were serviceable.

Our protectors provided us with changes of clothes, but they were only slightly more stylish than prison uniforms. Years ago, I wouldn't have minded, but now I did. I had become as fashion conscious as any CFC.

Because I hadn't been able to bring my computer, I couldn't do any writing. We had electronic devices for watching films or playing games, but no connection with the outside. However, the City Fathers who still had to run the world had assistants who visited regularly to update them on events and receive instruction.

Each family had a private suite with accommodations so basic it reminded me of military training camp—except we had no work to do.

Our duty was to mourn.

The CFC mourning protocol can be summed up in three words: follow the leader. The leader was the First Survivor. That's the spouse, if the decedent had one. If not, the oldest child, closest sibling, or so on throughout the legal order of succession.

The First Survivor sets the mood. Because Mimma wept quietly, loud wailing would have been an insult. If she'd bristled at the confinement and complained about the accommodations, it would have been permissible for others to do the same. Because she bore up stoically, however, we had to swallow our pride and make no objections. If she'd refused food, our provisions would have been scanty. But Mimma was the sort who turned to food for comfort.

In the usual scenario after a death, family and friends would come to the house. They would mourn with the First Survivor, attend to her needs, help with the legal arrangements. But this was not usual. Here, Mimma presided in an unfamiliar setting over more than a hundred mourners, most of whom were not related and whose ages ranged from the elderly Elip Hold down to the infant daughter of the Transportation Minister. But because the mourning protocol required it, we were all expected to interact as one big family. And that included eating together.

I wished Mimma had lost her appetite, as I did when I was upset. At the first meal, I was appalled at the quantity of food on the plate the server placed before me. Especially the steak. I opened my mouth to object, but Gray nudged me under the table. I glanced up at his stern face, and he gave an almost imperceptible head shake. In other words, I was to eat it and shut up.

My stomach didn't want all that food, and my mouth didn't want all that steak. I disliked the chewiness. My jaw was tired before I'd eaten half of it.

Not only did I have trouble chewing the meat, but worse yet, I couldn't digest it. As a result, nothing I put in my stomach at dinner was still there two hours later.

I've been through some unpleasant experiences, but mourning in forced isolation with a hundred CFCs ranks close to being buried alive. I was constantly sick, had nothing to relieve the monotony, and was surrounded by people whom I didn't like and who liked me even less, based on the looks of disdain they shot me when they thought I wasn't paying attention.

Besides all that, my sorrow was genuine. I felt the loss almost as keenly as Grey did. And his grief was crushing.

They brought the in body the second night, but we weren't aware of it until the next morning, when Father Hold announced that the minister was ready for viewing.

After breakfast, the ordeal commenced. According to City tradition, the minister was dressed in his finest and seated in an ornate death chair, posed with his hands on his knees. People whispered that the corpse artists had had to reassemble him, for the wave of automatic gunfire had cut his torso in half.

As if I wasn't already sick enough.

Mimma sat beside him in the matching First Survivor chair while we paid our respects. She seemed comforted by his presence.

No one else was.

Grey foundered in a sea of grief and confusion, not knowing how to swim in such waters. I wanted to comfort him, but I had no comfort to give.

Who had done this? Why? Why were we forced to stay here? There were no answers to our questions. No solidity to our world. What had once been our anchor was now a grim, giant manikin in Papa's clothing, shriveling, while we sought a new reality to believe in.

After many hours, Grey squatted before his mother's chair and took her hand. "Mimma."

Weak from illness and hunger, I watched from the doorway, wanting to help but not knowing how.

She patted his hand with her other, her marital bracelet catching the light. "He would want me to do something for their families."

"Pardon?"

"The men who died with him. There were six of them, I believe. They died in our service, trying to protect him."

"Yes, Mimma. They were good men."

"We must see that their families are made comfortable."

"It's being taken care of, Mimma."

She lifted her head. "Oh? But are their families still in pain?"

He stifled a sob. "I'm sure they are."

She raised her hand to his cheek. "What can I do to ease yours, Ashgrey?"

He shook his head. "Nothing, Mimma." He took her hand and kissed it. "But you've been here all day. You haven't eaten."

Nor had anyone else, except for the youngest children. When the First Survivor fasts, the whole family goes hungry.

Her expression changed like a gradual awakening. "Is it lunchtime? I haven't ordered anything for lunch."

"It's nineteen hundred, Mimma. Are you ready to eat something?"

Fresh tears sprang to her eyes. "Oh, my! Have I neglected my family? Has no one eaten all day?"

"We're fine, Mimma. I thought you might be hungry, is all."

She rose stiffly. "I shall have the kitchen prepare whatever they can make quickly. I should not have kept everyone waiting for so long." Holding Grey's steady arm, she took a couple of awkward steps. "Nor should I sit for so long."

An hour later, we gathered for sandwiches of thick bread stuffed with layers and layers of thin-sliced beef, with spiced autumnfruits and fried kartube slivers. The sides were delicious, but, hungry as I was, I could barely choke down my sandwich. I'd already had enough beef to last me a lifetime. But Grey's father loved beef, so for every meal, Mimma requested it in his memory.

Late that night, I rose to use the bathroom again and found Grey's side of the bed empty. After I finished my unpleasant business, I went looking and found him in the viewing room. Only one lamp was on, casting a dim glow. He had brought a chair near the body and sat across from his father as if in conversation.

I was struck by the resemblance between them. It was particularly eerie, because in that light, they both looked dead.

"There you are." I'd learned long ago to speak when I entered a room. Stealth came naturally to me, and if I waited until I was near before I spoke, it often startled people. "You weren't in bed."

He turned his tousled head. "Didn't mean to worry you."

"I knew you couldn't have gone far."

He rose and extended his hand. When I took it, he sat again and pulled me onto his lap. "Papa liked you." Arms around my waist, Grey laid his head against my chest.

I fingered his curls. "I liked him too."

"He wished you had called him Papa."

That was news to me. "He should have said something."

"He hoped you would do it of your own accord." The way he spoke in such precise City dialect, it sounded like a lofty accusation.

"I couldn't do that. It would have been an insult. To your father, that is. He was such a better a man than my papa, he deserved a better name." I rested my head on Grey's.

"I told him that."

"What did he say?"

Grey spoke so softly I could hardly hear him. "He didn't understand. How a man could reject his daughter. It would be like putting out his own eye. He couldn't fathom it." He hugged me tighter. "He wished he could have been a proper papa to you."

I had no answer to that, so I just kissed his head.

After a long silence, Grey asked, "What do you think happens when we die? What do they believe in Freemansland?"

"Nothing happens. We're just dead. Or do you mean burial customs?"

"No, I mean where is Papa now, do you think? The real Papa, the part that lives?"

I let out a long, slow breath while I considered how to answer. "The real Minister is sitting in front of you. There is nothing else. The part that once lived, lives no longer."

"No." He shook his head. "I don't believe that."

With sudden animation, he moved me from his lap, then stood beside me, holding my hand. "Look at that. It's an empty shell. Mimma takes comfort in thinking he's sitting there, but he's not."

He put his hands on my shoulders. "I feel your body, but I also feel the life in it." He took his hands from my shoulders, turned to the body in the chair, and grasped it the same way. "I feel his body, but there's no life. Feel it."

He grabbed one of my hands, dragged me over, and put my hand on one of the corpse's. "Feel that?"

I wanted to pull away, but a combination of fear of his mood and curiosity to understand made me unwilling to resist. "Feel what? It's cold. It feels dead."

"That's because there's no life in it. Now feel this." He took my same hand and clapped it onto the back of his own. "It's different, isn't it? And not just because it's warm, either. If I'd just had my hand in ice water, it would be as cold as Papa's, but you could still feel the life in it, couldn't you? A live body is alive because it has life in it. But what is that life?"

His actions were swift and jerky. The whites of his eyes glittered strangely in the dim light, and he was massive and strong and frightening. I tried to put a little distance between us, but he had a good grip on my hand.

"You're scaring me, Grey."

He let go and took a step back. "I'm sorry. I don't ever want to frighten you."

"It's this whole thing that scares me."

"Let's sit down." He took the chair we'd just vacated. "I need to talk. Is that okay? If we just talk?"

This was strange. He still scared me, but in a different way. "Of course we can talk. But I don't understand what you're saying."

That wasn't quite true. I perched on the edge of the chair beside his, uncomfortable, because I knew exactly what he meant. I'd observed the same thing as a child. You could pick up any small creature, even a woodlouse rolled in a ball, and tell if it was dead or alive. Even if it didn't move in your hand, you knew it either had life vibrating within it, or it didn't. The question was, what was that spark? The subject disturbed me.

"I'm talking about what some people call the spirit. You had spirits in Freemansland, didn't you? In your books, you talk about the spirits of the dead being in the mists floating over the stillwater, and the spirit people that haunted the woods."

"The spirits aren't *in* the mists. The mists *are* the spirits. But those are stories, Grey. Part of it's legend and part I made up. We didn't really have spirits in Freemansland any more than you do in the City."

When he didn't look convinced, I went on. "Just as it is with all those religions and things you used to study. People are looking for answers, and they come up with something that makes sense to them, that comforts them. But wanting to believe it doesn't make it true."

His brow furrowed. "I still do study it."

"You what?"

"I took my degree in the philosophies of religions because it fascinated me. It wasn't merely a cover for my IA activities. It was a field I would have gone into no matter what. You know that."

"I do." But I didn't like it. "I always liked your commander persona better. The professor was a bit weird, in my opinion."

"I'm sorry you feel that way, but the professor hasn't retired. He's no longer teaching but he's still learning. There are too many aspects to this world that science can't explain. Science can only address the physical, the quantifiable. It can't explain the soul."

"Possibly because there is no such thing. Did you ever think the life you feel in a living body is just electrical impulses? When the impulses stop, the life ends. I don't see why there has to be a spirit involved."

"But what shuts off the switch? And what starts the process to begin with? There must be a catalyst of some sort that sparks a body to life, some entity behind it all."

I had no answer to that. Should I even dignify such a ridiculous assertion with a response?

He draped his arms along the backs of the chairs on either side of him, reminding me of a gigantic night raptor spreading its wings. But instead of sending a spine-tingling call echoing through the night, he stared at me. The sensation it produced was just as unsettling.

I tried to meet his gaze, but I couldn't find it. His heavy brows shaded his eyes, leaving a dark, glittering hollow. His father's body seemed to watch us.

The hair on the back of my neck rose, and I stood. "I'm going back to bed."

"No, wait." When he took both my hands, he turned toward the light, and his eyes reappeared. They begged me to stay, and his hands squeezed mine in a plea for help. "I need you. I can't sort this out."

"And I can?" I remained standing for a few seconds, but when he didn't let go, I sat beside him again.

"No, I don't guess you can. I just need you with me."

"Do we have to be here? With..." I nodded toward the corpse. If I said, *with that*, he might be offended that I called his father an *it*. But I couldn't call it a *he*, for it wasn't his father. His father was gone.

Gone where?

Nowhere. He was no more. He'd ceased to exist. Why couldn't Grey accept that?

"Yes. He needs to hear."

I pursed my lips. "He's gone, Grey. He can't hear. You know he can't."

"I know he can't!" It came out in a cry. "All the things I wanted to say, but never did. I never told him I loved him. Never once."

"He knew you did. You showed him by the way you spoke to him, the way you treated him."

Grey slumped in his chair. "He was powerful. Everyone treated him with deference, even if they hated him. I was no different from anyone else. I feared him too. I showed respect, but never love. We never spoke of it. Neither of us."

"He knew you loved him." I leaned toward him. "And he loved you. You know how I know?"

He shook his head.

"Because he accepted me. As a City Father, he would never have welcomed a Freeman into his home. But his son loved me, and he saw me through his son's eyes."

Grey pulled me close and cried.

In the death chair, his father stared at nothing.

❧ Chapter 16 ❧

THE DRAGON

FOR A LONG time after Grey and I left the viewing room that night, he lay on his back, unmoving. I could tell from his breathing he wasn't asleep. I'm not sure what went through his mind, but mine was haunted with questions about spirits, life after death, the possibility that a realm existed apart from the physical.

I kept grabbing my thoughts and yanking them back to the concrete world. But in the dark silence of our room, I couldn't make them heel. The only way to control my thoughts was to speak them.

I just wasn't sure if that was advisable.

I moved close and laid my head on Grey's shoulder to whisper in his ear. "Are they listening to us, do you think?"

He didn't hesitate. "Um-hm."

So he thought this whole situation as strange as I. "Why?"

His hard, tense shoulder moved beneath me in a shrug. "I don't like the way the food makes you sick all the time. I know it's not proper for me to bring it up with Mimma, but this is going on too long."

That had nothing to do with my question, but figuring he had some purpose in mind, I went along. "No, you shouldn't say anything. I'll be okay."

"Every meal, we're given meat you can't digest. Mimma would put a stop to it if she were aware of it. We've never told her you can't eat hoofed animals, that the only meat your system can handle is birds or fish."

"Or rodents or reptiles."

He grunted. "We're not likely to be served any of those here."

"Please don't say anything. She'll feel bad. And anyway, this can't go on much longer, can it?"

"I don't know. But I do know *you* can't go on much longer, stuffing your stomach with food you can't digest and then losing it all. I hate to see you go through that. It's not good for you."

It wasn't. Not only did my stomach pain me, but I seemed to grow weaker by the day. "Let it go, Grey. That remedy I mix up with the bicarbonate, nimrel juice and fulamint oil helps. The kitchen staff's been nice enough to let me in there to make it. It's not a cure, but it helps me from getting too dehydrated."

"I'll see what happens tomorrow. If it looks like we're going to be here longer, I'll speak to Mimma."

The next day, Father Hold approached me after breakfast. "My dear, you look a bit wan. The rest of us grow fat with all this food, but you seem to be wasting away. Are you ill? Should we bring in a doctor?"

Could it be a coincidence that he'd mention it the day after my conversation with Grey? It was possible, of course, because when a person feels as bad as I did, it's likely to show. The kitchen staff might have said something as well. But the timing of his question was suspicious.

And the fact that when I stared at him, unspeaking, he showed signs of nervousness—rapid blinking and rubbing his fingers together—increased my suspicions. But he didn't look away, and his concerned smile never wavered.

"Thank you, Father Hold, but I don't need a doctor. It's just grief, the stress of the whole situation."

"Perhaps the food here disagrees with your Freemanslander digestion?"

I hoped my expression didn't reflect my thoughts, that he'd definitely been eavesdropping. "It's possible. But Mimma should order whatever she wants. I don't wish to complain."

When the server brought my plate at lunch, my suspicions were confirmed. "For you, ma'am." He set a moderately-sized serving of grilled pileti breast before me. "The First Survivor has requested that you be given poultry or fish rather than other meats."

Mimma looked toward me. "That is true, my dear, and I am so sorry to have not thought of it before. I knew you do not care for meat from a mammal, but I had no idea it was making you ill until Father Hold brought it to my attention." She turned to Grey. "Ashgrey, you should have said something sooner. It was cruel of you to let your wife suffer like that for no reason."

He lowered his eyes. "I am sorry, Mimma. We did not wish to bother you with our troubles."

"Well, that is just foolishness." Her stern expression softened when she addressed me. "Jemima, dear, I apologize for my thoughtlessness. Please be sure to let me know if I can do anything else for you."

"Thank you, Mimma. I accept your apology, though there's no need for it. And Grey and I are both more concerned for what we can do for you."

Her eyes filled. "Such a lovely girl." She pulled out a handkerchief and wiped her eyes. "Now, let us eat, shall we?"

I don't know what Grey was thinking—he didn't meet my gaze, and his face revealed nothing. But I had a few more questions to add to my ever-growing list.

⁂

MANY OF MY fellow "guests" in the compound acted like they didn't think a Freeman had any business being there, save perhaps in the capacity of servant.

The haughty ones included Grey's sister's husband. I liked Silver, but I could never figure why she'd married a man like Fenn Signet, the quintessential arrogant pigeonhead. Though he veiled his contempt with a thin film of politeness, he openly discouraged his wife and children from spending time with me.

On the fifth day, we paid our last respects to the minister. Though his body had been treated with the usual preservation chemicals, it was beginning to degrade, and Mimma agreed it was time to send it in for final processing. Before it was removed, everyone came to say goodbye, with the family sitting vigil.

Mimma sat beside him all afternoon, and Grey, Bark, and Silver took turns standing with her. We spouses sat across from them, along with the eldest of Bark's and Silver's children. The other guests filed through, offering words of comfort, praise for the minister, or memories of times they'd shared with him over the years.

After the last of the adults passed through, the younger children were brought in to say goodbye to Grandpapa. That was when Colaret, Silver's six-year-old daughter, came to me shyly. "Will you please tell us a story, Aunt Jemma?"

Fenn took her hand. "Now is not the time, Colaret. Come, leave the woman alone."

But the other children heard and came over too. "Are you going to tell a story, Aunt Jemma?"

Mimma had left her chair to stretch her legs. When she heard the clamor, she perked up and clapped her hands. "What a wonderful idea. Grandpapa loved hearing your stories. I think you should tell him one now, before he has to go." She sat beside the corpse again and patted its arm. "Jemima is going to tell the children one of her tales of Freemansland, dear."

She waved to the rest of the family remaining in the room, along with the mortuary team who had come to remove the body. "Sit, everyone. Papa wants to hear, and we shall all listen." She clasped her hands in her lap and smiled at me. "What is this story about, my dear?"

I had no idea. None of the story lines I had in mind for future books were appropriate for the occasion. But I couldn't turn down the First Survivor's request, and the children, even the older ones, seemed ready to hang on my every word. As I hesitated, Mimma motioned to Grey. "Pull a chair over here and sit beside me, would you, please, son?"

He did, and she took his hand, and all eyes turned to me.

The corpse's face was a macabre reflection of Grey's tortured expression. I gazed into my husband's dark, grave eyes and knew the story I would tell.

"There once was a boy who lived on Freemansland."

Several chairs to my right, Fenn stifled a snort.

"His father was a dragon hunter by trade. There wasn't much money in it, but he earned enough to feed the family. The dragons were good for food and for their hides. Have you ever seen something made from dragonskin?"

Bark's daughter's eyes glistened. "Mama has a dragonskin bag."

I nodded. "Dragonskin makes excellent leather goods, and the meat is good to eat. But dragons are dangerous, and if there are too many of them, they'll destroy people's homes and eat their children.

So dragon hunting was a noble profession. By killing dragons, this boy's father kept his own and many other families safe."

Bark's son, Tanstal, asked, "What was the boy's name?"

I hadn't thought that far ahead but said the first thing that came to mind. "Graybark. His name was Graybark." I met Grey's surprised gaze with a smile and continued. "The boy loved his father very much, but Papa was often away. He spent a lot of time looking for dragons. After he killed them, he had to skin them and preserve the meat, and then take them in his boat to the buyer, where he would bargain for the best price. He hunted other things too, and fished, so the family would have food to eat.

"Then one day, when Graybark's father was climbing on the sharpfall tracking a marshbear, a storm came up. The rocks grew very slippery, and Papa fell and broke his leg."

Little Colaret let out a cry and covered her mouth. "Is he all right?"

I nodded. "Once the leg healed, he could walk just fine. But in the meantime, he couldn't go dragon hunting. His family needed the money he earned, and after a few weeks, he heard dragons coming near their house. He had to kill the dragons before they killed his children, but with a broken leg, he couldn't do it alone. He needed help. So you know what he did?"

Wide-eyed, the kids shook their heads.

"He asked his son to help him." I felt Grey's eyes on me, but I didn't look up. "And you know what Graybark said when Papa asked?"

Tanstal hopped up from his chair. "I'll do it, Papa!"

"That's right. Graybark didn't know how to hunt dragons, but he knew his father did. And he knew his father wouldn't allow him to do anything he wasn't capable of doing. So Graybark and Papa got in the canoe and paddled off into the stillwater to hunt dragons."

As you've probably guessed, I modeled the story after my own experiences with my father dragon hunting—without the profanity, of course, and I changed some of the details. Everyone, child and adult alike, even the mortuary people, listened with rapt attention, gasping and chuckling and sighing in relief in all the right places.

Except for the minister, who only oozed an unwholesome odor. Beside him, Mimma's eyes glowed with delight, and beside her, Gray's eyes crinkled with a near-smile.

"That night," I finished, "when Graybark laid down on his mat, he was the happiest boy in the world. He'd learned much about life, and about work, and about death, which is part of life. But mostly, he was happy because he knew his papa was proud of him."

⁂

THAT NIGHT, WHEN Grey lay in bed, he pulled me close. "Thank you," he said.

"For what?"

"You know for what. For that story."

I shrugged. "It was just a story."

"But it was for me, wasn't it?"

I thought for a moment. "No. I think it was for all of us."

⁂

MIMMA HAD BEEN so distraught at seeing her husband's body wrapped up and taken away that she forgot to order a special meal for me. Steak was the minister's favorite meal, so that's what we all ate again.

As propriety dictated, I made no objection, and no one spoke up on my behalf, though Grey did give me a look of sympathy when the server set the plate in front of me.

He was sound asleep when I got up shortly after midnight, and I was careful to not disturb him. Without turning on the light, I put on my wrap and, after visiting the bathroom, made my way to the kitchen to mix myself a soothing potion of bicarbonate, nimrel juice and fulamint oil. How long were we going to have to stay here? And why were we really here, anyway? None of this made any sense, and I wished I could discuss it with Grey. But it was all too clear that there was no such thing as a private conversation in this place.

Moving in stealth mode was a lifelong habit, and no one could have heard me as I felt my way in the dark. I'd just stepped into the kitchen when I heard footsteps approach. Two sets of them.

I had good reason to be there, but by instinct, I darted into a recess between two ovens and crouched down. The footsteps drew closer, and voices spoke low. A few moments later, the kitchen lights turned on. I'd chosen my hiding place well, though, and unless someone looked for me, I wouldn't be seen.

"The real celebration can wait until we get home," Father Hold's voice said, "but this will do for now."

Two people passed through into the wine chamber, and I peered around the corner to see who was with the Father. I only saw the other man from the back, but I didn't recognize him. He wasn't one of the people confined here with us.

What were they celebrating? I heard mere snatches of the conversation until they came out of the chamber with a bottle. After that, I could only listen, for I didn't dare peek.

"Everything is in order?" the Father asked. "Every loose end snipped off or tied up? I do not wish to break into this two-hundred-year-old yusken until I am certain everything is perfectly in place."

"You can trust me, sir. The noose is around their necks, and we have covered our tracks completely." I didn't recognize his voice any more than I did his face.

I heard glasses taken out of the cabinet and set on the counter.

"Well, then—" Father Hold seemed to struggle with getting the bottle open. "I suppose after two hundred years, I should expect it to be sealed up tight, eh?"

"Just like the evidence we have planted. Sealed up tight."

The bottle was opened and drinks were poured. "I can scarcely believe it."

"Well, sir, believe it. It is true."

"You have no idea how long I have worked for this, to have that Standtall and his foolish version of integrity out of my way. Longer than you have been alive."

"I know that, sir. You are a very patient man, and I am happy to have been able to help you see it through at last."

"And now we can move forward."

They each drank, making appreciative noises. Then Father Hold chuckled. "You should have heard the story that Freeman woman told the children tonight."

"Sir?"

"Yes, she told them a story about a son helping his father hunt dragons."

"Did she really? How very interesting. I thought no one knew about me."

The old man's voice grew husky. "No one does, son. No need to worry about that. But it does seem to fit, does it not? We have slain the dragon together. And no one will ever be the wiser."

I closed my eyes and covered my mouth, willing my stomach contents to stay put.

THE NEXT MORNING as we assembled for breakfast, Father Hold went directly to Mimma. "Good news! Those who plotted against your dear husband have been apprehended."

I thought she was going to faint. Grey and Bark must have thought the same, because they each took one of her arms and supported her.

"Oh, my! Elip, who was it? Who could have done such a thing?"

The old man's expression was sorrowful. "We have followed the evidence carefully, and it is damning, though it is hard to fathom. The conspiracy was among our own. Land Forces General Rheta Denn colluded with General Pymon of Intelligence Acquisition. We have taken them both into custody."

Mimma sagged, and her sons helped her into a chair. "No! How can this be? I know Rheta and Stal did not see eye to eye on everything. In fact, he was very unhappy about the way she handled this Kenta business. But she was loyal. She was true. Or so we thought. And Fad Pymon? We thought him a good man. A good friend!"

People gathered around to comfort her until the young son of the Transportation Minister defused some of the tension by blurting, "Does this mean we can go home now?"

The minister clapped his hand over the boy's mouth, but Father Hold smiled wide. "It does indeed, young man! You are all out of danger. After breakfast, your papers will be returned, and you will be delivered back to your homes."

I couldn't wait to get alone with Grey—truly alone—and tell him what I'd overheard in the kitchen.

But the City was everywhere. Were we even alone in our own house?

❦ Chapter 17 ❧

GLASS PAINS

"THERE IT IS." I pulled my swimsuit from a drawer in the closet at our suite at Sentinel Pines. "I should have started looking from the bottom up instead of top down."

The suite door opened, and Grey spoke. "Did you say something?"

"Just talking to myself." I left the closet and found him in the bedroom dressed in a casual blouse and vest, trouser legs buckled at the ankles. "You're in hiking clothes. Are we going for a walk?"

"I was just coming in to tell you what Bark and I are up to." Embarrassment flashed across his face. "I guess you can come if you want—"

"I'd planned to go swimming, but walking is exercise too. I just need to move around after being holed up in that compound all that time."

He shrugged. "You can swim. I don't mind."

"Oh, so that's it." I made a face, pretending to be offended. "You don't want me around."

"Not at all. I said you can come if you want. But Bark and I wanted to—"

"You two need some brother time. I understand." I kissed him. "It's too cold out for me anyway."

"What do you mean? It's a perfect fall day."

"Too cold." I began removing my clothes to change into my suit. "The indoor pool is more to my tastes."

Aware of him just standing there, I looked up. "Did you want something?"

He smiled, his appreciative gaze wandering over my body. "Bark can wait."

⁂

ONCE RELEASED FROM protective custody, the family accompanied Mimma to Sentinel Pines to help her settle Papa's affairs.

I thought we might go back to the apartment off the clinic. We had, in fact, left some clothing and personal items there—such as my swimsuit—for when we visited. But Mimma, wanting us near, had our things moved into Grey's old room on the family floor.

We arrived late in the evening, exhausted from our long ordeal in the compound. But as soon we were alone in his old boyhood bedroom, I told Grey what I'd overheard the night before. I relayed the entire conversation, word for word.

He stared at me, his heavy brows lowered. "I don't understand. What are you saying?"

I glared back. He was supposed to help me make sense out of this, not ask for clarification.

When I didn't answer, he frowned deeper. "You must have misunderstood."

"Grey." I took his hands, and he allowed me to lead him to a settee. "I heard their conversation very clearly. I couldn't see their faces, but in the last several days, I've become familiar enough with Father Hold's voice to know who was speaking last night."

Grey shook his head. "It's not possible."

"I don't understand it either, but he and the man he was with are behind all this. They killed your father, Grey. They betrayed him, and your family, and the City."

"What about that other man? Who was he?"

"I don't know." That question consumed me as well. "Someone I've never met. From the way they spoke, he's Father Hold's son."

"Hold doesn't have any children."

"I don't know. I'm only telling you what I heard."

Despite the gravity of the situation, we didn't discuss it for long. It was too painful. Too unbelievable. Too exhausting. And I think we both half feared even these walls had ears.

⁂

OUR FIRST FULL day and a half at Sentinel Pines, we had back-to-back meetings with attorneys, accountants, and advisors. But when we gathered for lunch the second day, Mimma announced she would spend the afternoon resting alone in her room.

"You children can entertain yourselves, can't you?" She meant Gray, Bark, and Silver, who would always be children in her eyes.

Silver gave her mother a hug. "Of course, Mimma. Take it easy the rest of the day."

Bark radiated concern. "You're not ill, are you? Should we summon the doctor?"

Mimma shook her head. "No, dear. Not ill. Just weary." She patted his arm. "Nothing a stiff regimen of laziness won't cure. I'll just settle into my chair with a good book and a pot of babunja tea." She turned to me. "Jemima dear, you must write something for adults. Your children's stories are too short."

"I expect I'll do that one day. But I hope you won't read it with a cup of babunja, or you'll be asleep before you've gone five pages."

She gave a weary smile. "For today, that is my plan. When I read yours, I shall wish to stay awake."

Silver and Bark's wife, Pearl, took the children outside to play. Silver's husband, Fenn, hadn't come with us to Sentinel Pines, saying he had to get back to work. Bark and Grey went hiking. And I went swimming.

As Mimma had said, she was only weary, not ill, so we didn't have to call Dr. Genley for her.

We ended up calling him for Grey instead.

WHILE I SWAM and the children played, Bark and Gray walked the property, checking on the condition of the buildings and grounds. Grey carried a tablet and took notes.

Maintenance of the estate would be largely their responsibility now, as Mimma wouldn't keep a close eye on things. The estate steward, Starham, had been a faithful employee his entire life, and the brothers trusted him. But they wanted to take inventory with their own eyes.

I wasn't there, of course, but I heard the story from both of them later.

They checked out the bathhouse last. They shared a curiosity about that window they'd so often repaired, but they dreaded seeing it.

Once they'd made their way there, they examined the rest of the building before going around to the back. When they did, they found the whole window had been replaced. Not only new glass, but a new frame as well.

They stared at it, not speaking. The late afternoon sun angled through the trees behind them and turned the new glass into sparkling gold. The brothers squinted at the glare. And then, without saying a word, Grey put his fist through it.

THE CLINIC GREY'S parents had set up for my recovery at Sentinel Pines was still there. Dr. Genley sometimes used it to see members of the house staff or the grounds crew if they became ill or were injured, so they wouldn't have to go into the City for treatment. He was retired but lived near the estate and was always on call.

That afternoon, Grey lay on the exam table, eyes closed but fully conscious. I sat near his head holding his good hand, his left. His right arm was extended while Dr. Genley, assisted by a medical student, cleaned the wounds and picked out glass shards.

A nerve block took care of the pain, but there was a lot of blood. Though I'd never been squeamish, I couldn't watch what the doctor was doing.

It was good the injuries were to Grey's right arm, because he was left-handed. But the fact that it was his right made me angry, because it told me he'd done this deliberately. If it had been a thoughtless act, he'd have lashed out with his dominant hand.

Sitting there beside him, realizing he was out of danger—not bleeding to death, and with no permanent damage to tendons, apparently—my initial fear turned to fury. It took all my self-control to keep from screaming at him.

I bent and spoke low in his ear. "Your mother doesn't need this. She already has more than enough to worry about."

He didn't open his eyes. "You already said that. Three times, I believe."

I breathed slowly and deeply, trying to calm myself. "Let's make it four, then. As if we needed more trouble. What were you thinking?"

"I thought you were here to comfort me."

"I'm not sure what I'm here for." Hearing my voice rise, I modulated it. "What did you think you were doing, punching out that window?"

From the way Dr. Genley's assistant tossed quick glances between me and the doctor, I gathered he wished his superior would make me stop my badgering. But the doctor played deaf.

Grey still didn't open his eyes, but his face puckered. "I needed to fix it."

"What? The window?" My back kinked, and I sat up straighter. "And just how do you propose to do that now, with your hand and arm cut to ribbons? The maintenance crew did what your father instructed. They fixed the window after his death. Do you really think he wanted you to turn around and break it? What do you think he'd have to say about this?"

"Just stop." His voice turned sharp, and tears trickled from the corners of his eyes. "I don't need you rubbing salt in the wounds."

Grey's mention of salt, in combination with the blood I was seeing and the horrors of the past week, brought me back to my own papa's dragon skinning shed. I tasted the salt in my mouth, felt the burn in my eyes. It was as if my head were stuck in a barrel, and my blood chilled at the remembered sound of Ibro's cruel voice, the savage grabbing of his horrible hands.

The world faded into black.

"Mrs. Standtall?" Dr. Genley's voice wafted through a fog. "Can you hear me?"

⁂

DR. GENLEY HAD already summoned an ambulance for Grey. When it arrived, he put me in it too. "Whenever a patient loses consciousness, I like to have them checked out," he explained. "Especially since you hit your head when you fell."

And especially when the patient has brain worms, is what he didn't say. But I heard him thinking it. Though the family may not know of my condition, he did, for I was his responsibility during my convalescence at Sentinel Pines. He always seemed wary around me, as if I might shape-shift into a slavering, glowing-eyed ghoul any moment.

The emergency vehicle was large enough to accommodate all three of us—Dr. Genley rode along to see to our care and keep the family apprised of our conditions. At the hospital, he ordered tests for me and then assisted the surgeon who stitched up Grey, leaving me to fend for myself while awaiting the results.

All my tests came back negative: no concussion from the fall, no change in brain worm activity. But the hospital kept us both overnight. Me, for observation, and Grey, because he'd lost so much blood and they wanted him to rest.

On the ride back to the estate the next day, I didn't know what to say to Grey as he stared out the window, brooding and silent. I kept far enough away that I wouldn't accidentally bump his arm as I allowed the passing scenery to absorb my attention.

After forty minutes or so of silence, I came out of my private reverie. When I turned toward him, he looked away. He'd been watching me.

The layers of wrappings around his arm made it look twice its usual size. His hand was covered with a thick mitt of bandage, and the whole thing was in a sling. Remembering what it had looked like before they'd covered it, I shuddered. "How are you feeling?"

After a pause, he answered, still facing the window. "Foolish. No, more than foolish. Imbecilic."

"Is that even a word?"

He turned to me then, which was what I'd been shooting for. "If it isn't, it should be." His grimness smoothed a bit as he eyed me. "How are *you* feeling?"

"Like I wish I could hug you, but I don't want to disturb your arm. That's got to hurt."

He shrugged. "No more than one could expect from multiple lacerations, some to the bone."

"So it's just kind of vaguely uncomfortable, huh?"

"I don't really know. I'm so full of pain meds I'm not sure what I'm feeling. Other than foolish. I'm pretty clear on that."

Careful not to jostle his arm as I reached toward him, I stroked his cheek. "Imbecilic, you mean."

He grabbed my hand with his good one and kissed my fingers. "Yes. That's what I mean. And you were right. My father would not have wanted me to do that."

"Though perhaps he would understand why you did it." I paused. "But I don't. I think it was idiotic."

Grey frowned. "You're supposed to be supportive. You should have said, 'No, Grey, you're not an imbecile.'"

I gave him a sweet smile. "I might, except we promised to be honest with one another."

⁂

THE FOLLOWING DAY, the mortuary called to let Mimma know the remains were processed and ready for delivery. Father Hold and the new Minister of Domestic Peace asked permission to present them. Did the Widow Standtall have any objections?

Of course she didn't. She would be honored. She set the Presentation date for early the next week and invited any of the extended family who could, to come.

We had no breakfast that day, nor dinner the evening before, for the tradition was to fast before the Presentation. When we dressed for the event, I had to ask Silver to help me, as Grey was unable to fasten the long line of twenty tiny buttons going up the back of my floor-sweeping charcoal mourning dress. As for Grey, his shirt was blousy enough to go over his bandages, but there was no fitting that arm into his coat. He wore it with one side draped over his shoulder covering the sling. As long as you didn't notice his hand comically mittened in bandages, he cut a striking figure.

Though I'd read about the Remains Presentation, my research indicated that each family did it a little differently, so I didn't know quite what to expect. Unfortunately, Grey's somber mood discouraged me from asking.

Somber fails to convey the depth of his gloom. He'd been quiet since the news of his father's death. But once I told him what I'd learned about Father Hold, he was like a krymperslug living along the edges of the stillwater. When injured or alarmed, a kymper will close in on itself, shrinking to a third of its normal size and bristling with sharp scales. Grey hadn't shrunk, but he was deeply withdrawn and definitely bristly.

Therefore, my only preparation for the event was when Grey tossed me a paper that appeared to be torn from a book. I thought it was a poem until he ordered, "Learn this. We're going to sing it."

Singing? At a Remains Presentation? The lyrics seemed to be snippets of nonsense joined together with barely discernable threads of logic. I learned them, though, and figured I'd pick up the melody as we sang.

We joined the family in the receiving hall at the time appointed. With Mimma's and the minister's siblings and cousins, we numbered forty-three altogether, including children. Young and old alike wore the prescribed mourning garments, which I've heard referred to as the uniform of grief. They were uncomfortable things, with coarse fabrics and tight bands holding everything close to the skin. The intent was to remind us of our sorrow. As if there was any danger of our forgetting.

The Presentation is particularly hard on young children. In order to keep them properly quiet and somber, their parents traditionally spanked them before entering the receiving hall and promised them worse if they didn't behave perfectly. From the terror I saw on the children's faces, the Standtall family upheld that practice.

The little ones sat, quiet and wide-eyed, while the adults remained standing—except for Mimma, who sat in the First Survivor chair. We each approached to greet her, then moved aside and spoke quietly with one another.

As the number of mourners increased, so did the tension. When one of the young relations giggled, his father took him out and refreshed his pain quite thoroughly, from the sound of it. That ratcheted the strain up a notch or two, but it did encourage the rest of the children to keep still, especially after the boy was returned, tear-streaked and hiccoughing.

The room's temperature rose. Clothing chafed. The polite murmuring waned to a miserable silence. Mimma sat with sober patience.

Was this supposed to drag on so long? What we were waiting for?

And then the estate steward, Starham, stepped through the doorway and bowed in Mimma's direction. "Madam, I like to announce the entrance of the esteemed City Father, Elip Hold, accompanied by the new Minister of Domestic Peace, Janren Stock. The chief mortician is with them."

She nodded and rose. "Thank you, Starham."

We all turned toward the doorway. In walked the mortician in mourning dress, followed by two Ministry Security guards in their standard black suits, followed by Father Hold in charcoal gray, closely trailed by...

...the man I'd seen in the kitchen with Father Hold that last night in the compound.

Janren Stock was the secret son of Father Hold? He had conspired with the Father to assassinate Stal Standtall. And now, he stood in the receiving hall of the Standtall estate, bearing the box containing my father-in-law's remains.

I wanted to launch myself across the room, pick up one of the pieces of statuary sitting about, and smash his face with it. But I stood tall and serene, breathing slowly and calmly, and smoothed my expression into one of quiet mourning.

I couldn't keep myself from trembling, though, and gripped Grey's good hand with both of mine.

If he was aware of my agitation, he didn't show it.

I WAS SO FURIOUS with the esteemed Father and his illegitimate minion, I don't know how I got through the Presentation without exploding.

I watched, seething, while the chief mortician, Father Hold, and Minister Stock offered their condolences to Mimma. She sat again, and Grey disengaged himself from me so that he, Bark, and Silver could take their places beside her chair.

Minister Stock held the box. The chief mortician opened it and pulled out a double string of black beads—all that was left of my father-in-law. His remains had been processed and formed into the little globes, which then were dipped in glass to preserve them and strung on an unbreakable altago chain.

The chief mortician handed the beads to Father Hold, who approached Mimma and put them around her neck. As he fastened the clasp, he mumbled the prescribed empty words of comfort. *Your beloved husband will be with you always in a bond than cannot be broken,* and that sort of nonsense.

The chief mortician reached into the box again and removed a chain with a tiny key hanging from it—the key to her marital bracelet. He handed it to Mimma. "From your husband's heart to yours."

She put the chain over her head and tucked the key into the bodice of her mourning dress. "I shall never unlock my bracelet. He put it on, and it shall stay where he put it."

The chief mortician bowed. "As you wish, ma'am. That is your right."

"And I will exercise it." She reached over and took Silver's hand, then sought the gaze of Pearl and me. "Remember this, daughters. When we truly love our husbands, that love endures beyond death."

I glanced at Grey beside her, but he didn't look my way. The chief mortician closed the box, and Minister Stock handed it to Father Hold, who presented it to Mimma. "For storage of the beads, madam." The cover was carved with a likeness of my father-in-law as well as his name.

"Thank you, Father Hold. It was very kind of you to take the time to come and make the Presentation. I can't tell you how much this means to me."

I gritted my teeth. Oh, there was so much I wanted to tell him!

The chief mortician turned to the rest of the people in the room. "You may now approach and see the remains."

That invitation initiated a parade of the family past Mimma once again, this time to admire the box, finger the beads, and kiss Mimma's cheek. After that, they left the room one by one.

We in the immediate family concluded the procession, then escorted Mimma out of the reception hall and into the entry foyer where the others waited. Outside, the wind howled and sleet hammered the windows overlooking the dreary grounds and the skylight overhead.

Custom dictated that the next phase be conducted outdoors, there being some idea about the deceased's spirit leaving the box and going free into the air. I shivered at the thought of going out in that kind of weather. Mimma must have agreed, because she stayed in the foyer.

Standing beneath the dreary skylight, she opened the box and held it in both hands. Her brother and sisters gathered around with a hand on her shoulder or back. Their spouses held the free hand of their respective wife or husband. The minister's sisters put their hands on the box, denoting their connection with the deceased, with their spouses grasping their free hands.

Mimma's children then took the shoulder of one of the aunts or uncles—Grey chose Uncle Cago Talpin, the Minister of Agriculture—but his other arm was out of commission. So instead of taking his hand, I grasped his shoulder and lifted my brows in a silent question. *Is this acceptable?* He made a sober nod, then turned back toward his mother.

The remaining children, grown and otherwise, joined in the same fashion until all were connected to one another through Mimma and the box representing her husband. The chief mortician, Father Hold, and Minister Stock stood by and watched.

When everyone was in place, the chief mortician began to sing. "We are children of the Fathers who once have saved the world."

The family took up the song. "We are fathers of the children who will keep its ravel purled. We are married to the Fathers who make it all run true. We are mothers to the children whom the noble blood runs through."

The tune was simple enough to follow, even if I couldn't quite grasp what we were singing about. Perhaps you had to be a CFC to find it meaningful. As we sang, Mimma turned in a slow circle in time to the music. We shuffled in a spiral about her, hanging onto one another and almost tripping over each other. I appointed myself guardian of Grey's injured arm, making sure my body was always between it and everyone nearby.

The song was nonsense. Our clothing constricted. Our movements made less sense than the song. We were weak from hunger. I couldn't see any of the children, but the one time I heard a whimper, it was quickly cut off—by what means, I didn't know.

I'd been through some pointless exercises in the past, particularly in military training. But never had I participated in anything so ridiculous as this. The man was dead. What was the purpose in prolonging our own suffering? Freemansland traditions were a whole lot more reasonable. When a person died, we wasted no time. Within twenty-four hours, he'd be rolled in a net and tossed into the Stillwater, where his soft tissue would be eaten by the fish, and his bones would become one with the mud. Those who remained then got on with their lives with hardly an acknowledgement that anything had changed.

Because there really was no change, was there? We come and we go, just like those who came and went before us. The events of the world continue in their never-ending cycle no matter who gets on or falls off. Nothing changes.

The song repeated until we'd made one complete turn. We continued to cling to one another until the chief mortician concluded with, "And so we move on, and carry the world on the combined strength of our shoulders."

Standing in place, we repeated the phrase, then we disconnected from one another.

It was nonsense. Pure nonsense. No one carried the world, not even the broad-shouldered Standtalls. We were all helplessly tossed about. Just when we thought we could climb out of the stillwater, a dragon would grab and drag us back in. We'd scale the sharpfall only to slip and crash downward. As often as we rose, we'd fall again, until we rose no more.

Better to be drowned at birth and be done with it.

❧ Chapter 18 ❧

THE VOW

WET SNOW DROPPED in grim clots as the autocab pulled up in front of our apartment building. Dez, the doorman on duty that afternoon, hurried to open my door, and I stepped out.

Grey exited on the other side, moving gingerly. The pain meds didn't seem to be doing their job. But when Dez tried to assist, Grey raised his hand. "No need for you to help. But thank you."

"Welcome back, Mr. Standtall, Mrs. Standtall." The doorman made a little bow. "The place hasn't been the same without you." He raised his brows. "You have no luggage?"

Grey shook his head. "We were hurried out with nothing, and we return the same way. And thank you, Dez, for your kind letter of condolence. It was a lovely gesture."

Having two hands, I was in charge of the tip card, and I rummaged for it in my bag as we hurried through the bone-chilling damp and into the building. "Yes, Dez. It meant a great deal to us. You're a dear." I handed him the card.

"Multiply by fifty," Grey told him.

The doorman's brows rose. "You needn't, sir—"

"No, we need not, but we want to. It's a small expression of how much we value your service."

He scanned the card and keyed in the multiplier. "Thank you, sir. You are most generous."

We had a similar conversation with the elevator operator.

Neither man asked about Grey's arm. Did they already know what had happened, or were they trained to not ask questions? Probably both.

Once inside, Grey pulled a small device from his trousers pocket. "It's good to be home. Does it smell musty, do you think?" While he spoke, he used the tool to sweep for listening devices.

"Maybe a little stale." I went to the aquarium. "Glad to see the fish have been cared for properly while we were gone." I ran my finger along the top of the wainscoting. "And the cleaning people have been keeping up with things."

"In the front room, at least. I'm going to check the rest of the house."

I tagged along, making small talk while he did the sweep. "How's your arm?"

He shrugged. "It'll heal."

"You should ask the doctor to change your pain meds."

"Why?"

"They don't seem to be helping. You don't complain, but I can see you're in pain. I'm surprised, considering the powerful prescription you're on."

"I haven't taken anything since I left the hospital."

"What? Why not? It wasn't making you sick, was it?"

"It was making me numb."

"Isn't that the point?"

He didn't answer as he finished the sweep. Then he tucked the device away in the back of a desk drawer. "We're okay for now. But we should check it again next time we've both been away."

I wanted to argue with him. To say, "That's crazy. Who would sneak in and plant microphones?" But under the circumstances, I said, "Where'd you get that? Do you even know it works?"

He nodded. "It works. I tested it. And never mind where I got it."

"It's not going to help, you know." I took his good hand, led him into the media room—his favorite part of the house, not counting the bedroom—and sat on the big chair. It was barely big enough for the two of us, so sharing it was nice and cozy. "Not taking your pain meds, I mean." I patted the seat beside me, and he sat, adjusting the sling so his bandaged wing could lie along the chair arm.

"What do you mean? What's not going to help?"

"You people seem to think physical pain can make the inner pain go away, the way you torture yourselves during mourning. And worse yet, you torture your children. How can you do that? Did your parents do that to you? Starve you and beat you when your grandparents died?"

"You mean preparing the children for the Presentation? I suppose it seems harsh if you're not raised that way. But death is painful, and children need to learn to treat it with proper respect."

I shook my head. "I'm talking about the fallacy of inflicting pain to relieve pain. It simply doesn't help."

He narrowed his eyes. "What are you trying to say?"

"Punching out that window, and now denying yourself medication, isn't going to change anything. Your father was murdered by the government you trusted. It's beyond tragic, both losing him, and the betrayal by the people you once held in high regard. I could see torturing *them* for what they've done, but why cause yourself such pain? For such an intelligent man, you sure can be stupid sometimes."

Despite being one-armed, he launched himself out of the chair and turned to face me, red-faced. "Stop it! Don't say any more!"

I stood too. "Why not? Somebody's got to say it. You're being foolish, Grey. Foolish to think you can change anything. The world is a terrible place, and it's full of terrible people. It's always been that way and it always will be. We need to get on with our lives. Let the wicked ones do what they want. We can't stop them. We should just keep out of their way and live our lives as best we can."

"No." He shook his head. "No. Listen to me—"

"No, Grey, listen to *me*. I didn't tell you before, because I was waiting for a time and place I thought was safe. But you know that conversation I overheard in the kitchen at the compound? When I overheard Father Hold talking to that other man, the one I didn't know?"

He scowled. "Yes. And I don't want to believe it. I've known Father Hold all my life. The thought he might be behind Papa's murder makes me sick to my stomach. But I've seen enough to know something's amiss here, and I don't deny that you heard what you heard. I just don't know what to think of it."

"Yes, it's hard to fathom, even for an outsider like me. But it's worse than you know. I've found out who the other man was. The secret son of Father Hold who's in conspiracy with him."

Grey's eyes widened. "Who is it? How do you know?"

"Because I saw him. This very afternoon, I saw him, and I recognized his voice. It's Janren Stock."

Grey jerked as if jolted with electricity. He turned away, running the fingers of his good hand through his hair and breathing heavily, but saying nothing.

I circled around to face him as he stood with bowed head. "I'm so sorry about all this, Grey." I put my hand on his shoulder. "I'm sorry I shouted at you just now. I shouldn't have said you were stupid. You're not. Far from it. I only said that because I'm scared."

He lifted his gaze, his expression dazed. "What?"

"I was scared all the time as a kid. I got over it for a while, especially since marrying you. But now, I'm more afraid than I've ever been in my life. Then, I was frightened of what I didn't know. Now, what I *do* know scares me more than the unknown ever did."

He put his one arm around me and drew me close.

"I need you, Grey. That's why I've been so upset with you. Because I almost lost you just when I need you most. I need you to have two arms to hold me."

"I'm sorry, Freeman." His voice was soft and husky. "But this is bigger than you and me."

Whatever he was getting at, I was pretty sure I didn't like it. I sought comfort by burying my face in his chest—except that gliching sling was in the way. That made me angry with him all over again. I wanted my whole Ashgrey back, not this awkward, maimed version.

He seemed oblivious to my distress. "When I said I wanted to fix it, I wasn't talking about the window."

I didn't say anything. He wasn't of a mind to hear me anyway, so why bother?

"That is, I did mean the window." He spoke in clipped, precise CFC speech. "I had planned to repair it myself, with Bark, and I was upset to see it had already been done. But that was only representative of the real issue."

He rested his cheek on my head. "I should have seen the plot against my father. Now I realize I *did* see it, but failed to understand. I did not fit all the pieces together in time to see the picture they were forming until too late. I should have seen it."

I lifted my head and looked into his ashen face. "You couldn't have. They're at the top level of government. They know how to cover their tracks."

"But I know my business as well. Or I thought I did. I should be on top of these things. My father is dead because of my negligence."

I took a step back. "That's not true, and you know it. Don't ever say that again. Don't even think it. He's dead because those murderous betrayers killed him. They framed innocent people to take the fall, and they beat you and everyone else at Stealth in the process. None of that is your fault. They're wicked people, Grey. And wicked wins sometimes. A lot of times."

I'd never seen his expression so distraught. But a moment later, his face hardened, and I'd never seen it so grim.

"I need to fix it." He pulled me back into his one-armed hug. "I *will* fix it." He kissed my head. "I swear on the death beads around my mother's neck. I. Will. Fix it."

❧ Chapter 19 ❧

IN DEEP

TWO MONTHS LATER, we returned to Sentinel Pines for Mimma's birthday.

At first, she'd borne the loss of her husband with stoic courage. Now, reality had set in full force. Though in her grief she preferred not to celebrate her birthday, all her children and grandchildren came to see her anyway. We just didn't have a party.

When Grey and I arrived, the sodden weather served as a fitting backdrop for the somber mood. I remembered the first time I'd seen the estate, all aglitter with fresh snow. Now, the snow that had fallen earlier in the season slouched in sullen disappointment, beaten into submission by near-freezing rain and cringing into the cold, bare ground.

I talked with Silver in the hall outside our rooms when Bark's oldest, Willow, approached and greeted us with hugs. "Where are Spenn and Colaret?"

Silver put her arm around her niece. "Oh, I am sorry, dear. I know how all you cousins enjoy getting together. But they had obligations at school and were unable to get away."

Willow's face fell. "Really? My parents told our school we were going to see our grandmother, and they let us go without question."

"I'm disappointed too." Silver spoke quickly, as if in a hurry to change the subject. "But you'll see them at the New Day holiday. So I hear you got to visit your dad on the set of the new movie he's working on. What was that like?"

"Oh!" Willow clapped. "I got to meet Ando Green!" She put the back of her hand to her forehead in imitation of a swoon. "He is *such* a god! And he gave me his private messaging code!" Her hand dropped to her side. "But Daddy won't let me use my personal account to message him. Why does he think I need a chaperone for *everything?* Even personal *messages?*"

Silver smiled. "Because he's your father, hon."

I couldn't speak for fathers, but I did know Bark. "And because he loves you."

Willow frowned. "Well, I wish he could love me from more of a distance. Didn't you aunties hate it when your papas interfered with your friendships?"

Silver and I exchanged glances. Then she said, "I suppose I did at the time. Now, though, I realize he always wanted the best for me. To protect me as long as he could."

Her manner was sorrowful. She still grieved her father's loss, of course, for it had only been a couple of months. But was there something more going on?

Willow turned to me. "How about you, Aunt Jemma? Was your papa super-controlling like that?"

What could I say? My papa tried to kill me at birth?

"When I was your age, I didn't have a father."

"Oh, Aunt Jemma, that's so sad!" Willow seemed close to tears. My niece KJ's emotions fluctuated wildly too. Were all young girls like that? Perhaps my giddy fellow students at Freemansland Academy had been more typical than I'd thought.

"You have a good family," I told Willow. "But no matter how good we have it, life doesn't always seem fair."

She pouted. "It sure doesn't. Do you think—" A sly smile crept across her face. "Could you talk to my dad about letting me message people without him looking over my shoulder? He has so many blocks on my account, about the only person I can talk to without his permission is Grandmama."

I laughed. "Well, then, enjoy talking with her."

"I intend to do that right now," Silver said. "But in person, not in a message. Come with me?" She looked back and forth between the two of us.

I shook my head. "I'll be along later. I need to see what Ashgrey's up to."

Willow sidled up to Silver. "I'll go with you. Would you talk to Daddy for me? He's your brother, he'll listen to you."

They continued their conversation—a fruitless one, from Willow's point of view—and I returned to our suite. Grey was in the sitting room, clothes changed and waiting for me to get back, frowning at the screen of an old-fashioned lap computer.

I gave it a curious glance as I approached. "Looks like you're ready."

He blanked out the screen before I saw what was on it. "I've been ready. Where have you been?"

"I told you, I was talking to your sister. You could have come get me, you know."

He set the computer on a nearby table. "I could, but then I found this old thing. When I had it at school, it was cutting-edge stuff. Seems rather quaint now, doesn't it?"

"I'm surprised it still works."

He rose and offered me his good arm. "Let's go see Mimma."

The stitches were removed from his hand and arm, but the wounds were still tender and horrible to look at. When out in public, he wore a thin glove on his hand and a protective sock-like thing over his arm, though at home, he left it uncovered.

Now that he was mostly recovered, however, he wasn't home much. Until he reappeared to make this trip with me, I'd only seen him four days of the last twelve.

I wrapped both my arms around his as we walked down the hall. "Your mother grieves so. I'd like to do something for her, but I don't know what. How can we help her?"

"Seeing the grandchildren should cheer her, I think. And the rest of us. But mostly the children."

Children. The word struck with a familiar hollow thud in my middle. Children were a promise I could neither receive nor deliver.

HOW HAD I ever thought Citizens First Class had no troubles?

But I need to tell you about Silver. I hinted earlier that I thought something was amiss, and I was right. After observing that she acted distracted and seemed to favor her left side, my investigative instincts prompted me to look for a way to speak with her alone.

It wasn't easy. I finally had to bother her after she'd retired for the night.

A short time after we'd left Mimma and gone to our respective suites, Grey went to shower, and I told him I had to talk to his sister about something. I slipped out of our room and knocked on her door. "Sorry to bother you, Silvie. It's Jemma. Do you have a minute?"

I heard movement inside, and after a few moments, the door opened a crack. "What do you need?"

"Nothing. It's just— do you mind if I come in?"

She stepped back, and I entered. The suite looked like a girl's room, just as Grey's looked like a boy's. The fact their parents hadn't remodeled after their children left home touched me.

"I don't want to butt in," I said.

"It's okay." She hadn't undressed yet, but she had removed her make-up, and she looked haggard. "Come in and sit down." She led the way to the settee. "What's going on?"

I'd been looking for a way to approach the subject discreetly but couldn't come up with one. "I'm concerned."

Her demeanor turned wary. "About what?"

"You know I'm a trained observer, and after working as an investigator for ten years, those old habits are hard to shake."

She watched me, listening but not interrupting.

"Tell me to go away and mind my own business if you want. But is something wrong?"

As she studied me with her deep, dark eyes, I saw flashes of both her mother's stately beauty and her father's quiet strength.

"I should tell you—" She took a breath. "To mind your own business, as you said. But you're family. So I suppose that makes it your business."

I hoped my expression revealed the genuineness of my concern.

She sat straight on the settee and folded her hands. "Fenn and I are—having problems."

I didn't say anything for a moment. I didn't want to pry, but I had to ask. "Did he—hurt you?"

She lowered her head and stifled a sob.

I leaned forward and held one of her hands. "I'm sorry, Silvie. I shouldn't have said anything. But I couldn't help but notice—"

She shook her head but didn't look up. "No, I'm glad you did. It's a terrible secret to bear. I can't tell Mimma. But I'm so afraid—"

"How long has this been going on?"

"A couple of years." She reached for a tissue on the end table. "He's never touched me when anyone's around. And he never—well, once. Only one time did he leave a mark on my face." She wiped her eyes. "I pretended I was ill and canceled all my engagements until I was healed enough that makeup could cover it."

"Oh, Silvie! But—why didn't you come home? Didn't you and he sign that non-violence agreement?"

She nodded but cried too hard to speak at first. When she finally got out a sentence, it was, "I was afraid of Papa."

I didn't understand until she added, "What he would do to Fenn."

Images of the smoldering rubble of Kentak flashed through my mind. "I see your point. But—"

"And now, I can't bear to tell Mimma. She would be terribly upset. I promised to leave the first time he struck me. You know that, you promised the same thing. And I didn't keep my promise. And that means—because I failed to fulfill my part, he can't be prosecuted. We're both in violation of the agreement."

Next moment, she was sobbing in my arms. What was I supposed to do? Her shuddering seemed to cause her pain, and I was afraid to hold her tightly for fear of hurting her. "You need to tell her, Silvie. You can't let this go on."

She nodded in my embrace. "I know. I know. But how can I?" She pulled back and wiped her eyes on a fresh tissue. "Jemma, I'm so ashamed! How can I tell her?"

"I'll go with you," I heard myself say. Why? I wanted nothing to do with this. "Let's go right now, before you lose your resolve." What I meant was, before I lose mine. I stood. "Come on. We should catch her before she's in bed."

Silver grabbed my hands and pulled me back down. "Give me a few minutes. I need to put my make-up back on."

"She's your mother. She's seen you in your bare skin, so she won't be shocked at your bare face."

Silver blew her nose. "Oh, this is so hard."

"It's got to be better than going back to him."

She shook her head. "I can't go back. Not after—no. I can't go back."

"Tell Mimma. She'll know what to do."

She took slow, shallow breaths, as if the effort was painful. "Yes. Yes. You're right." She turned frightened eyes to me. "You will come with me, right?"

I nodded. "Yes. I'll come with you." I stood again and offered her my hand.

≈∭≈

LATER, WHEN I told Grey what I'd been doing all that time, he took it as hard as I expected.

He strode back and forth. "How badly did he hurt her? Why didn't I see it?"

"Her bruises are all hidden by clothing. But there are a lot of them, and they're pretty bad. Dr. Ganley's coming tomorrow to take a look, but we think she might have a cracked rib."

If not for the fact that his hand wasn't healed, Grey might have punched a wall. He had plenty of things to say, though, none of it nice, and I sat on the bed hugging a pillow, legs drawn up, and kept out of the way. I answered questions if he asked, but mostly, he ranted. He was angry with Fenn, to be sure. He was upset with Silver for putting up with it as long as she had. And he was angry with himself. I'd seen there was something troubling Silver, but he hadn't picked up on it.

Why did he think he should know everything?

Though I didn't worry about Grey turning on me, his anger was terrifying. He tended to be intense even at rest, but once riled, he was a sight to see. Or more like a thing to hide from. I wanted to defuse him but didn't know how. When I couldn't take it anymore, I slipped from the bed and sought refuge in the bathroom.

I didn't quite make it before he spied me and stopped his pacing. "Freeman, where are you going?"

I shut the door and locked it. "I have to go to the bathroom."

"Is that all?" He was outside the door. "Are you okay? You looked scared as a mouse in a corner when you got off the bed."

"What am I supposed to look like when you're tearing around the room like a madman?" I thought I'd been taking it all fairly calmly, but my voice—and apparently my mousey face—told a different story.

The doorknob rattled.

His voice was incredulous. "You locked me out."

"I'll be out when you settle down."

"I'm settled. Don't lock me out."

"I'll open it in a minute. I can't reach it right now."

"Freeman, don't lock me out. I won't hurt you."

At least he didn't try to open the door again. I stared at it, though, wondering if he'd pick the lock. "Give me a minute."

It sounded like he slumped against the door. "Hurry up. I need you."

I flushed and washed my hands. Which were shaking. I dried them slowly.

He must have been listening for me to unlock the door, because as soon as I did, I heard his weight remove from it. He was standing out there ready to—to what? I wasn't worried about him hurting me. Was I?

I opened the door slowly.

His face was strained with agony. He opened his arms. "I'm sorry. I didn't mean to frighten you."

I went into his embrace and held him tightly. "I wasn't afraid you'd hurt me. I just can't stand seeing you that way."

He mumbled things I only half understood about being sorry for frightening me, for not protecting his sister, for being so foolish as to put his fist through the window, for—

I stiffened in his arms. "Ashgrey. Would you stop it already?"

He pulled back. "What?"

"Just stop it."

He dropped his arms and stared. "But she's my little sister. And that Fenn, he needs to be—"

"It's bad, yes. But Silvie's finally done the right thing and told Mimma. Your mother will see to it. It's taken care of."

"But Mimma's grieving. She—"

"Your mother needs someone else to think about instead of herself. You should have seen her tonight. Once she saw her daughter was in trouble, she rose to the occasion."

"You're not saying it's good this happened—"

"Of course not. But Silvie's finally getting help, and Mimma's feeling useful again. It's a tough time for your sister, but she's got her mother to help her. And she'll be here to help Mimma with all she still has to deal with. They'll find strength in each other."

After staring at me open-mouthed, he shuffled to the bed and sank onto the edge of it. "Freeman, you amaze me."

I sat beside him. "Why?"

"You're so brave. So sensible. When something bad happens, I try to shove it out of the way. But I can't move it. I only end up hurting myself. But you? You stare it down until you see the way through. And then you just—" He swept his hand in a forward motion. "You just plow through the center of it. You get to the other side and look back. It's behind you. But I'm still trying to fight it." He shook his head. "How do you do it?"

I shrugged. "When you're thrown in over your head, you can't move the water. You either learn to swim through it or drown." I gently stroked his mangled hand. "I learned to swim early on."

❧ Chapter 20 ❧

INTO THE CLEAR

WHEN I WAS frightened as a child, I hid in the wilds of Freemansland alone. I did the same now, through my writing. But this time, I wasn't helpless. I controlled all that was, all that happened, the course of my characters' lives.

I cared little for historical accuracy. Before the City barged in, Freemansland's records were sparse at best. Few cared to memorialize our history then, and fewer still cared to research it now. So I shaped the world as I saw it, mixing truth with conjecture and salting it with might-have-been and wish-it-were.

As I wrote for progressively older readers, each story grew more serious. More complex.

Scarier.

I lived in a rather narrow world. Most of my social contacts were fellow writers or others in the publishing business. We'd get together to talk about life, writing, and the writing life.

I befriended some of my neighbors, and I sometimes met one or more of them to swim or walk together, or have lunch. Every once in a while I'd go visit Jeriah and his family in Saltcreek Point. But mostly I stuck to myself. And that was the way I liked it.

Grey had been gone a lot before his father's death. Afterward, we were apart sometimes for weeks on end. Sometimes with little to no contact. In his absence, I immersed myself in writing.

The sitting room was my favorite place to work, facing the aquarium. I'd look at the little model of the six-tiered island, watch the fish swimming and the fronds of foliage swaying, and mentally slip into the stillwater with them.

It was an escape, but also an anchor, a tangible reminder of Grey's love. I drank in the sight of it when he seemed only a sweet memory. I lived in his house, in his name, on his money, but the aquarium reminded me I was no usurper. He had brought me here because he loved me and wanted me to feel at home.

Did he know, when he arranged to have this aquarium installed, that he would so seldom be here with me? I didn't believe that was what he'd planned, but it was the way it played out.

I was pretty sure he didn't spend all his time on official Ministry Security business. His vow to "fix" things was not made lightly, and I had no doubt some of his investigations took him places the new Minister of Domestic Peace would not want him to go.

My occasional sweeps of the house for listening devices never turned up anything suspicious. But even in the privacy of our home, it was best some things remained unsaid.

MY GAZE FOLLOWED a pair of silver crestfin performing their sinuous mating dance around the aquarium. I lost sight of them when they slipped into the effigy of Freemansland to complete the process in the relative dark.

It bothered me how much I'd like to complete that process myself.

No wonder the fish were feeling amorous—the sun had gone down and the city lights sparkled on the other side of the window. A beautiful scene.

I rose and stifled a moan. Though it wasn't unusual for my pelvis to ache this time of the month, it hadn't been this bad for a long time.

To give the fish the right ambiance, I hobbled to the aquarium and shut off the light. Their efforts would prove fruitless, for the tank's other residents would eat the tiny hatchlings within an hour of their appearance. But at least the lovers could enjoy their pointless exercise.

I looked out before closing the drapes and shutting myself in. Almost every night for eight years, I'd surveyed that glittering cityscape. Eight years.

Forefinger hovering over the control switch, I murmured, "Goodnight, Centre City. If you see my husband out there somewhere, tell him I miss him." I pressed the button, and the heavy drapes whirred along their tracks toward one another until they met with a click.

The fish joined in the tank, the drapes joined on the wall. Where was *my* other half?

There was a time when I'd thought of Jeriah in those terms, though ours was an altogether different sort of union. We were, nevertheless, like two parts of one entity. If anything happened to him, I was pretty sure my heart would stop beating as well. I couldn't imagine how I could go on without knowing he was out there.

I wiped my eyes with my fingers. Hormones didn't usually make me so emotional. I hated it. It was bad enough that my bones ached and my womb wept over its emptiness every four weeks. I didn't need my eyes flowing too.

I wasn't surprised when my phone sang out with Riah's jaunty ringtone. I'd been thinking about him, so he must have been thinking about me.

I shuffled to the kitchen where I'd left the phone—my version of hurrying when my hips felt like this—and picked it up. "Hey. How'd you know I needed to talk?"

"Hey." His voice sounded strained.

"You okay?" I switched to video mode and moved into the dining room. "Put me on picture." I eased myself into a chair and set the phone on its holder.

Riah's face came into view. It was as strained as his voice.

I gave what I hoped was an encouraging smile. "What's going on? You look like a honey pile."

"Thanks. You alone?"

"I was, until you called. How about you? I don't hear the kids. They off somewhere?"

They weren't little anymore—KJ was a teenager, and Jeo's voice was starting to change—but I could frequently hear them in the background when Riah and I talked.

He put his face in his hands.

Something like panic rolled over me. "Riah? What's going on?"

He didn't lift his head. "They're gone." It came out like a sob.

I almost leaped from the chair. "What? Jeriah, what are you talking about?"

"I'm such a slotting idiot!" When he lifted his head, his face was twisted in agony. "She left me, Jem. She took the kids and went back to Freemansland."

"Seena? She did not. She hates Freemansland. She'd never—" I stopped. "No. Don't tell me." I stood. "She'd never go back unless you gave her a reason. Okay, tell me." I picked up the phone so I could yell at him without bending over. "What did you do, Jeriah?"

He looked off to the side. Couldn't look me in the eye, even on camera. "Nothing I haven't been doing for more than ten years. She just found out about it, is all."

"Jeriah…" I spoke through clenched teeth. "You slotter! You are a filthy, sliming— you've been cheating on Seena for over *a decade?*"

He turned back to me, frowning. "I'm not proud of it, but, well, slime. What am I supposed to do? I travel a lot, you know? And—"

"And she waits for you at home, and raises your kids, and keeps your house immaculate, and cooks like an award-winning chef, and you *cheat on her?*"

I guess I did get pretty shrill—my shriek kind of echoed in my ears. But that didn't give him justification for what he said next.

"And you think your husband doesn't?"

SAID HUSBAND RETURNED the next day at mid-morning. I was still in bed. Not sleeping. I simply didn't want to get up.

When the front door opened, I lifted my head, not sure what I'd heard. I was reaching for the weapon in the nightstand when I heard his voice on the far side of the apartment. "It's me, Freeman."

I dropped my hand and wilted back onto the sheet. It wasn't him I was upset with.

"I tried calling you, but you didn't answer."

I didn't now, either.

"Where are you?" His voice drew nearer.

His footsteps entered the room, bringing the rest of him with them. "Are you sick?"

I rolled over and looked up at him. "Not really." The sight of his anxious face revived me a little. "I almost forgot."

He sat on the bed. "To get up?"

"No." I elbowed myself to a half-sitting position. "I was thinking about that but was too lazy to actually do it."

When he bent to kiss me, I wrapped my arms around his neck and pulled him all the way down.

"I almost forgot how good you look in the flesh. I see you so seldom these days, you've almost become an imaginary friend."

He'd recently taken to the latest trend of wearing only a mustache, no beard, and I stroked his bare chin with my thumb. "I forgot about your missing whiskers, too."

"I thought you didn't like them." He pulled his long legs onto the bed and stretched out beside me.

"I don't like it bushy, because it hides your handsome face." My hand moved from his smooth jaw and along his neck to the broad swath of tiny pleats across the front of his shirt. "This is new too."

"I've had this shirt a few weeks. You sure you're not sick? Because I don't want to catch it if you're contagious."

"All I've got is a foul mood."

I rested my head on his shoulder and he ran his fingers along my back. "I won't catch that from you, but maybe I can infect you with my good mood." His hand went lower. "What do you think?"

"You'll have to wait a few days, if you're thinking what I think you're thinking."

"Oh." He sighed. "Well, I expect to be home for a while." He sat and swung his legs off the bed. "You must be deep in the dumps. You didn't even yell at me for not taking my shoes off."

I rolled over and covered my head with the pillow. "Take your shoes off."

From the sound of things, he did. "So why didn't you answer your phone?"

"It's broken."

"What?" He yanked the pillow off and tossed it on the floor. "How am I supposed to hear you when you talk into a cushion?" He leaned over me. "Why didn't you answer my call?"

"I need a new phone. It's broken."

"How'd you break it?"

"I got mad."

"As in angry?" He sat on the bed. "At whom?"

"My brother. To whom I shall never again speak. Nor of. Nor so much as utter his contemptible name. He is dead to me."

"What happened?"

And so I told him. Replayed the highlights of the shouting match, culminating with my declaration that he was no longer my brother. "'I'm never speaking to you again,' I screamed. 'And don't call me, because you won't reach me. See?' And that's when I smashed the phone with the pepper mill."

Grey listened, his expression unreadable.

I pounded the bed with my fist to demonstrate smashing the phone. "And then I cried."

He took me in his arms.

"And I cried all night. And I haven't stopped." Actually, I had, but I'd started again. "And I'm not going to talk about it anymore, so don't ask me." I grabbed a tissue and made a show of blowing my nose.

"All right, I won't ask. But I will tell you something."

I turned away. "I don't want to hear it."

"A lot of men cheat on their wives, and probably as many women are unfaithful to their husbands."

"I'm not listening. I'm through with this subject." Though he'd tossed my pillow on the floor, the bed had plenty more. I pulled another over my head.

He yanked it away despite my death-grip on it. "We are not those people."

I covered my head with my arms. Not as good as a pillow, but they were available.

"Have you ever been unfaithful to me?"

I turned and glared at him from between my crossed arms. "No! Of course not! How dare you suggest that? I am not—I'm not the person we're not talking about anymore."

"Neither am I. So why are you worried that I might have been unfaithful to you? We are not those people. Neither of us."

I narrowed my eyes. "I know *I'm* not."

"Until last night, had you ever had doubts about me?"

I considered. "No. Never."

"So why are you wallowing in misery all morning? Get up and get dressed, and let's go get you a new phone." He stood and offered me his hand.

I let him help me up. "I'm not going anywhere without a shower."

"That's good, because I'm not taking you anywhere without a shower."

As I got out clean clothes, he kept talking. "I'm very proud of you, by the way."

"For what? Breaking my phone with a hard object instead of my hand?"

"That too. But I was referring to the fact that when I came home and found you in bed, you didn't smell like booze or dead fish."

I paused in the bathroom doorway. "Oh. Yeah. Well, I came closer than you know."

"But I do know. I've been talking to Raig."

I turned and went into the bathroom. "Oh." Raig was the doorman on duty last night. "Why were you talking to him?" I closed the door.

Grey stood outside and answered through it. "I met him as he came back from walking the Blynes' furball, as he does every morning."

"Yes, he does. Since when does a doorman double as a pet walker?"

"Since he's infatuated with Mrs. Blyne. Anyway, he told me what you did last night, and he wanted me to thank you for your generosity."

I turned on the water, shouting, "I can't hear you anymore."

He entered the bathroom. "I'm just passing along his thanks. And adding my own."

What was I supposed to say? "Oh. Whatever."

"I'll thank you more appropriately when I can, but I just want you to know. What you did last night means the world to me. I love you more every day, but this morning, I love you twice as much."

"You do not. You're being ridiculous."

"Perhaps you're right. It's hard to measure love. But I intend to pour some out for you. Do you have anything you need to do today? Or can I take you out on the town?"

"I have no pressing deadlines, if that's what you mean."

"It is. Well, then. I'll make some arrangements while you get ready."

You're probably wondering what he was so pleased about, so as I finish my shower, I'll tell you.

After my shouting-match with the slimy gel eel whom I shall not name, I was spent. I ached all over, inside and out. I wanted to crawl inside a bottle and never come out. Ever. With you-know-who out of my life forever, and my husband absent and probably in another woman's arms even as I sat in the dining room quivering—envisioning that possibility, I gave the phone a few more hearty thwacks, which failed to remove the image from my mind—I had nothing to live for. Nothing.

So I got on the Beverage Bureau's site. They offered all-night delivery. My mouth watered—yea, my mind begged—for that Shade Shadow whisky I used to get lost in. I didn't even care that the price had skyrocketed since the last time I'd bought it, which was several years ago now. Two hundred fifty urexi, plus twenty for delivery, was well within my means.

After his father died, Grey let the Bureau ban expire, and now I could buy liquor whenever I wanted. Funny thing was, I never did. I could have sat in the house all day and all night drinking my brains out, and Grey might never have known. But the only time I had so much as a glass of wine was when I was with other people. I didn't trust myself to drink alone.

Until that night. That night, I planned to drink myself to death or die trying. So I ordered the Shade Shadow, to be delivered immediately. The after-hours order added another thirty urexi. That brought it to three hundred a bottle. I could afford it. Especially since I was going to be dead soon. If the whisky didn't kill me, Grey would.

I waited impatiently for it to arrive. How long could it take to deliver a bottle across town?

Long enough for me to have second thoughts. That's exactly how long.

I went downstairs and found Raig at his station. "I ordered something from the Bureau," I told him, "but I've changed my mind. I don't want it after all." I handed him an envelope. "Would you be so kind as to give this to the courier? Then keep the delivery for yourself. You don't even need to let me know it's here."

He blinked at me. "I beg your pardon, ma'am?"

"Do you drink whisky?"

"On occasion…"

"Well, then, you will have some next time the occasion arises." I waggled the envelope. "This is for the courier."

Still looking confused, he took it and slipped it into his breast pocket.

"And this is for you." I handed him my tip card. "Double it, since you're going out of your way for me. And you can do whatever you want with the bottle when it comes. Drink it, give it away, sell it, whatever you want." I smiled. "Just don't drink it on the job."

He stood at attention, and I thought he was going to salute. "No, ma'am!" He grinned. "Thank you, ma'am. My parents' fiftieth anniversary is coming up, and I've been looking for something special to bring them."

"Good. This is special. Are you familiar with Shade Shadow?"

His smile widened. "It's the old man's favorite! When he worked over at the Trenmar Towers, one of the gentlemen there used to treat him to some every now and then. He still talks about those days. If I could give him a bottle of Shadow, he'd kick up his heels for sure, ma'am."

I was amazed at how excited he was. Doormen weren't usually so talkative.

So why did I decide not to drink myself to death that night? Because as I waited for the delivery, I stared at the aquarium, and in my mind, I swam with the fish in the murky stillwater.

But the waters weren't murky. They were clean. They were well and expensively tended to. Nothing dead floated in them. The fish in the stillwater would have looked at their counterparts in my aquarium and said, "What did they do to deserve such a life?"

The answer? Nothing. Just as I did nothing to deserve this good life of mine. Grey simply gave it to me because he loved me.

He loved me.

He was not my brother. He was my husband. And he took that responsibility seriously. It wasn't naive of me to think he was faithful. It was realistic.

I was my brother's sister, but I was no longer a Freeman. I had no desire to muddy these crystal clear waters.

Nope. Not a Freeman. My last tie to that world had just been cut off. I would pull myself up and stand tall.

End of Book 2
Jemma's story concludes in Book 3, *Free*

If you enjoyed this book, please let the world know with a review on Amazon, Goodreads, and/or your own blog. Readers and authors alike always appreciate reviews.

Thank you!

Telling "the old, old story" in surprising new
ways…

Yvonne Anderson writes
fiction that takes you out of this world

Fly through the **Gateway to Gannah**
for some serious sci-fi adventure

Book 1: *The Story in the Stars*
(Finalist, ACFW Carol Awards, 2012)
Book 2: *Words in the Wind*
Book 3: *Ransom in the Rock*
Book 4: *The Last Toqeph*

Also, check out "First Love," Anderson's novella in
Coming Home: A Tiny House Collection
Seven stories from seven authors featuring
characters who live in tiny houses.

www.YsWords.com